Mooney, Carla
The Creators and Cast of Glee

Jay Stream Middle School

The Creators and Cast of Glee

by Carla Mooney

LUCENT BOOKS
An imprint of Thomson Gale, a part of The Thomson Corporation

GALE
CENGAGE Learning

Detroit • New York • San Francisco • New Haven, Conn • Waterville, Maine • London

Jay Stream Middle School

© 2012 Gale, Cengage Learning

ALL RIGHTS RESERVED. No part of this work covered by the copyright herein may be reproduced, transmitted, stored, or used in any form or by any means graphic, electronic, or mechanical, including but not limited to photocopying, recording, scanning, digitizing, taping, Web distribution, information networks, or information storage and retrieval systems, except as permitted under Section 107 or 108 of the 1976 United States Copyright Act, without the prior written permission of the publisher.

Every effort has been made to trace the owners of copyrighted material.

LIBRARY OF CONGRESS CATALOGING-IN-PUBLICATION DATA

Mooney, Carla, 1970-
 The creators and cast of Glee / by Carla Mooney.
   p. cm. -- (People in the news)
 Summary: "This series profiles the lives and careers of some of today's most prominent newsmakers. Whether covering contributions and achievements or notorious deeds, books in this series examine why these well-known personages garnered public attention"-- Provided by publisher.
 Includes bibliographical references and index.
 ISBN 978-1-4205-0789-8 (hardback)
 1. Glee (Television program)--Juvenile literature. 2. Television actors and actresses--United States--Biography--Juvenile literature. I. Mooney, Carla. II. Title.
 PN1992.77.G5558M66 2012
 791.4502'80922--dc23
 [B]
                                                                2012002243

Lucent Books
27500 Drake Rd
Farmington Hills MI 48331

3 3752 00876 7383

ISBN-13: 978-1-4205-0789-8
ISBN-10: 1-4205-0789-3

Printed in the United States of America
1 2 3 4 5 6 7 16 15 14 13 12

Contents

Foreword	4
Introduction	6
A Successful Musical Comedy	
Chapter 1	9
Building a Breakout Show	
Chapter 2	23
The Lynchpin	
Chapter 3	35
The Driving Force	
Chapter 4	46
The *Glee* Club	
Chapter 5	59
The Cheerios	
Chapter 6	72
The Jocks	
Notes	85
Important Dates	95
For More Information	97
Index	99
Picture Credits	103
About the Author	104

Foreword

Fame and celebrity are alluring. People are drawn to those who walk in fame's spotlight, whether they are known for great accomplishments or for notorious deeds. The lives of the famous pique public interest and attract attention, perhaps because their experiences seem in some ways so different from, yet in other ways so similar to, our own.

Newspapers, magazines, and television regularly capitalize on this fascination with celebrity by running profiles of famous people. For example, television programs such as *Entertainment Tonight* devote all their programming to stories about entertainment and entertainers. Magazines such as *People* fill their pages with stories of the private lives of famous people. Even newspapers, newsmagazines, and television news frequently delve into the lives of well-known personalities. Despite the number of articles and programs, few provide more than a superficial glimpse at their subjects.

Lucent's *People in the News* series offers young readers a deeper look into the lives of today's newsmakers, the influences that have shaped them, and the impact they have had in their fields of endeavor and on other people's lives. The subjects of the series hail from many disciplines and walks of life. They include authors, musicians, athletes, political leaders, entertainers, entrepreneurs, and others who have made a mark on modern life and who, in many cases, will continue to do so for years to come.

These biographies are more than factual chronicles. Each book emphasizes the contributions, accomplishments, or deeds that have brought fame or notoriety to the individual and shows how that person has influenced modern life. Authors portray their subjects in a realistic, unsentimental light. For example, Bill Gates—cofounder of the software giant Microsoft—has been instrumental in making personal computers the most vital tool of the modern age. Few dispute his business savvy, his perseverance, or his technical expertise, yet critics say he is ruthless in his dealings with competitors and driven more by his desire to maintain Microsoft's dominance in the computer industry than by an interest in furthering technology.

In these books, young readers will encounter inspiring stories about real people who achieved success despite enormous obstacles. Oprah Winfrey—one of the most powerful, most watched, and wealthiest women in television history—spent the first six years of her life in the care of her grandparents while her unwed mother sought work and a better life elsewhere. Her adolescence was colored by pregnancy at age fourteen, rape, and sexual abuse.

Each author documents and supports his or her work with an array of primary and secondary source quotations taken from diaries, letters, speeches, and interviews. All quotes are footnoted to show readers exactly how and where biographers derive their information and provide guidance for further research. The quotations enliven the text by giving readers eyewitness views of the life and accomplishments of each person covered in the *People in the News* series.

In addition, each book in the series includes photographs, annotated bibliographies, timelines, and comprehensive indexes. For both the casual reader and the student researcher, the *People in the News* series offers insight into the lives of today's newsmakers—people who shape the way we live, work, and play in the modern age.

Introduction

A Successful Musical Comedy

The television show *Glee* is a musical comedy about a group of eager and ambitious students who are trying to shine onstage and survive high school at the same time. The show debuted in 2009 and features an ensemble cast of many unknown, but talented young actors. It centers on Will Schuester, a young Spanish teacher at the fictional William McKinley High School, who takes over the high school's struggling glee club, New Directions. The show follows the glee club's preparations for the show choir competition circuit, which involves dancing, singing, and costumes. It also delves into the students' relationships and issues as they are bullied by the school jocks and shunned by the popular kids. In each episode the cast performs about half a dozen songs. With its irresistibly catchy beat, *Glee* single-handedly made high school glee clubs cool in schools across the United States.

Glee quickly became a pop-culture phenomenon. Its style is unlike anything seen on television before. It developed a loyal fan base of "*Glee*ks," who tune in each week to share in the music, laughter, and drama. In its second season, *Glee* attracted about 10 million viewers each week and was the number-one scripted hour among teens and adults, ages eighteen to forty-nine. The show has received several prestigious awards and honors, including Emmy Awards, Golden Globe Awards, a Peabody Award, and a People's Choice Award. Its cast has also been recognized. In 2010 actress Jane Lynch received an Emmy Award for her performance as cheerleading coach Sue Sylvester. In 2011 Lynch and her cast

With its cast of previously unknown but talented performers, elaborate production numbers, and creative use of music, Glee has become a pop-culture phenomenon.

mate Chris Colfer received Golden Globe Awards for their performances. In his heartfelt acceptance speech, a stunned Colfer dedicated his win to "the amazing kids that watch our show and that our show celebrates and are constantly told no [by] people and environments and bullies at school, that they can't be who they are or can't have what they want because of who they are."[1] The cast of *Glee* performed for President Barack Obama at the White House, appeared on the *Oprah Winfrey Show* (1986–2011), graced numerous magazine covers, and embarked on two sold-out summer concert tours. The show has also become an international phenomenon, broadcast in countries around the world.

In addition to being a critically acclaimed television series, *Glee* has revolutionized the way music is presented and sold.

Its unique take on modern hits and classic show tunes made the show one of the hottest music properties in the world. *Glee* has two Grammy Award nominations, music sales of millions of albums, and more than 33 million digital song downloads. *Glee* even surpassed the Beatles for having the most songs on the Billboard Hot 100 simultaneously. The cast's version of "Don't Stop Believin,'" a song written and first performed by the rock band Journey, has sold over a million digital copies. "The cast of *Glee* has truly reinvented our song for their generation," says musician and songwriter Jonathan Cain, a member of Journey. "It is rare when a song that is over two decades old can be a new sensation again. We are honored."[2]

Other musicians have taken note of the show's unique promotional platform. When the cast's versions of their songs air on the show and hit the charts, the original versions and musicians also benefit from increased sales and exposure. The effect has been so noticeable that even legendary artists like Paul McCartney are contacting the producers about having their music included in the show.

Glee is a successful combination of a traditional musical and a weekly television show, and it appeals to the geek in everyone: jocks, cheerleaders, braniacs, and people with disabilities. The show works hard to tackle contemporary issues that affect young people, such as teenage sexuality, body image, bullying, and divorce. "*Glee* presents this idealized world where no matter who you are or how different you are from the 'norm', you're going to get supported in this glee club," says Lynch. "And you're going to be held up as unique, and you're going to be loved for it. Also, raising your voice in song is one of the most courageous things you can do. And I think people really respond to that."[3]

Chapter 1

Building a Breakout Show

On May 19, 2009, the pilot for a new television show called *Glee* premiered on the FOX network. Show creators Ian Brennan, Ryan Murphy, and Brad Falchuk anxiously watched and wondered how viewers would react to the show. In the world of television programming, it is hard for a new show to stand out. Networks cancel plenty of good shows before they have a chance to find fans. Yet the three men believed that *Glee* had something special, a quality that would set it apart from other shows.

Ian Brennan

Ian Brennan knew as a teenager that he wanted to be an actor. He joined the show choir at Mt. Prospect High School in suburban Chicago, Illinois, to help him land roles in the school's musicals. "The show choir director was also the musical director. If you wanted to be in the musicals, it helped if you were also in the show choir. So I joined,"[4] Brennan explained.

Brennan enjoyed being onstage, but show choir was not his favorite activity. He recalled,

> I didn't particularly find it enjoyable, and it still strikes me as weird that people dress up in sequins and perform song-and-dance numbers. But, at the same time, I find it interesting that there is something in everybody, a longing

Creator Ian Brennan based his idea for Glee on his own experiences as a member of a high school show choir.

for something transcendent, particularly in a place like Mt. Prospect, a place that's very suburban and normal and plain. Even in places like that, there's this desire to shine. That's fascinating and very funny to me, especially when people try to accomplish this through show choir—which, to me, is inherently a little ridiculous.[5]

Brennan went on to attend Loyola University Chicago, and after he graduated, he began his acting career with the prestigious Steppenwolf Theatre Company in Chicago. He later moved to

New York and performed in a few off-Broadway plays. Brennan never forgot his days in the Mt. Prospect show choir. He thought that life in a show choir could be a great story, so he decided to write a movie screenplay.

Brennan, however, was an actor, not a writer. He had dabbled in some writing, but nothing as big or as challenging as a movie screenplay. "I'd read a lot of screenplays, but I'd never written one,"[6] he admitted. In the summer of 2005, Brennan bought a book titled *Screenwriting for Dummies* and sat down to write. About a month later, he had completed the screenplay.

For two years, Brennan offered his script to movie studios, but no one was interested in buying the show choir concept. Then Brennan got lucky. A friend belonged to the same gym as television writer and director Ryan Murphy. Murphy was well-known for creating the television series *Nip/Tuck* (2003–2010). Brennan's friend offered to give Murphy a copy of Brennan's script. "As it turns out, Ryan grew up in Indiana and had been in show choir through college, which is hilarious. So Ryan came back and said, 'I get this world,'"[7] said Brennan.

Ryan Murphy

Ryan Murphy understood the show choir world that Brennan featured in his script. Growing up in Indiana, Murphy sang in a church choir. He also performed in several high school musical theater productions. These experiences helped him relate to the world in Brennan's script.

After graduating from college, Murphy took a job as an entertainment reporter for the *Miami Herald* newspaper. He later wrote for other newspapers, including the *Los Angeles Times* and the *Washington Post*. Murphy usually wrote about celebrities and the business of Hollywood. Eventually, he realized that he wanted to be part of the entertainment industry instead of just writing about it. He spent nights writing his first movie script, *Why Can't I Be Audrey Hepburn?* "I sold that script to [director] Steven Spielberg, and that started my career. It just sort of happened. It was very sort of miraculous and easy is the wrong word because [I] guess

Veteran writer, producer, and director, Ryan Murphy, joined the Glee team after the run of the popular television drama Nip/Tuck, which he created.

that I had been preparing for that moment all along. But I literally just sort of wrote it, sold it, and fell into it and have never stopped working since,"[8] said Murphy.

Even though Murphy's first script was never made into a movie, it helped him break into Hollywood. In 1999, Murphy jumped into television as the creator and producer of the teen comedy, *Popular* (1999–2001). The show aired for two seasons but never gathered a mainstream following. Murphy kept working, writing a comedy screenplay titled *St. Sass* that aired as a TV movie in 2002 on the WB network. He also directed and wrote the short film *Need*, which was shown in 2005 at the Mill Valley Film Festival,

12 The Creators and Cast of *Glee*

an annual independent film festival in California. Murphy then directed and produced the film *Running with Scissors,* which was released in 2006. He also wrote the screenplay. The film stars Annette Bening, Alec Baldwin, and Gwyneth Paltrow.

A journalism assignment led to Murphy's most well-known work before *Glee.* In order to write an article about plastic surgery in Beverly Hills, Murphy posed as a potential client at a well-known plastic surgeon's office. He intended to write a sarcastic look at how people made ridiculous changes to their bodies. Yet at the appointment, Murphy found himself wondering what surgery could do for him. "I left that meeting, that consult with the plastic surgeon, and A, I didn't write the article; and B, it sort of threw me because he really made me feel that I would have a happier, better life if I would just sort of work on what he deemed my physical imperfections,"[9] said Murphy.

Even though he did not write the article, the meeting gave Murphy an idea, which he turned into a television series about two plastic surgeons called Nip/Tuck. Murphy even used the real surgeon's question, "What don't you like about yourself?" as the show's signature line in each episode. The series was an immediate hit. In 2004 Murphy won an Emmy Award for Outstanding Directing for a Drama Series for the pilot episode. In 2005 Nip/Tuck won a Golden Globe Award for Best Television Series, Drama. It ran for seven seasons, ending in 2010.

Glee Is Born

In 2003 Brad Falchuk joined *Nip/Tuck* as a writer, and he and Murphy formed a close friendship. Together they wrote a pilot for a TV series about transsexuals called *Pretty/Handsome.* The show was never picked up by a network. As *Nip/Tuck* neared its end, Murphy and Falchuk began to look for a new show idea. After the dark themes and graphic surgeries on *Nip/Tuck,* they hoped to find something lighter for their next project. "I've been doing very dark material," said Murphy. "I was interested in expressing something other than depravity."[10]

The timing was perfect for Murphy and Falchuk to read

Building a Breakout Show 13

Writing *Glee*

For *Glee's* first two seasons, Ian Brennan, Ryan Murphy, and Brad Falchuk wrote the scripts for all twenty-two episodes. Often, they would meet one night a week at a local restaurant and talk about the next episode that they needed to write.

To write an episode, the three decided on the episode's basic theme or premise. Then they started brainstorming and pitching ideas to each other, eventually developing the ideas into a simple story line. Next, the writers divided the story out into acts and wrote scenes. Brennan wrote most of Sue Sylvester's scenes, while Falchuk wrote many of Kurt Hummel's scenes, with Murphy providing input. The writers then put the scenes together to form an episode, cutting parts that did not work, adding jokes, and finding songs that fit the story.

In 2011 *Glee* hired six writers to join Brennan, Murphy, and Falchuk for the third season.

Brennan, Falchuk, and Murphy wrote the scripts of the show's first two seasons as a team.

14 The Creators and Cast of *Glee*

Writer Brad Falchuk helped Brennan and Murphy transform the original Glee screenplay from a movie to a television format.

Brennan's show choir script. It was exactly what Murphy and Falchuk were looking for. Murphy believed that the concept would work best as a television series, instead of a movie. He talked to Brennan about revising his screenplay into a television series. Brennan agreed, and the three men sat down to entirely rewrite the screenplay into a television show.

The trio decided that the show would be a one-hour comedy set in a high school in the midwestern town of Lima, Ohio. The show would follow Spanish teacher Will Schuester, who suddenly finds himself coaching the school's struggling glee club. Each episode would have five to seven songs, chosen from a variety of musical genres. There would also be strict rules as to when characters would sing. "I wanted to do a postmodern musical. [The FOX network] was not interested in, and neither was I, doing a show where people suddenly burst into song. I said, 'Look, if they're going to sing, there are going to be three rules: It will be

Building a Breakout Show **15**

done where they're on stage rehearsing or performing, in the rehearsal room, or it will be a fantasy that is rooted on the stage,'" said Murphy. None of the show's songs would be original. The cast would perform well-known songs by other artists. "I was very inspired by [the television show] *American Idol* because I think the key is to do songs that people know and interpret them in a different and unusual way,"[11] explained Murphy.

FOX Signs *Glee*

Murphy and Brennan approached the FOX television network with their series idea. FOX already had *American Idol* (2002–), a hugely popular reality television singing competition. "It made sense for the network with the biggest hit in TV, which is a musical, to do something in that vein,"[12] said Murphy, and he was right. FOX executives loved *Glee*. They agreed to the show fifteen hours after receiving the script.

Despite the enthusiasm, everyone involved with *Glee* knew that a musical television show was a risk. Previous attempts at musical television produced flops, such as *Cop Rock* in 1990 and *Viva Laughlin* in 2007. Successes like *Fame*, a show about a high school for the performing arts that aired from 1982 to 1987, were rare.

The cast of Glee gathers for a screening of the pilot episode on May 11, 2009, a week before the show launched on Fox following the season finale of American Idol.

The Pilot Premieres

FOX executives decided to tap into *American Idol*'s popularity to introduce *Glee* to viewers. They scheduled *Glee*'s pilot to air on May 19, 2009, immediately after *American Idol*'s season finale. *Glee*'s first season, however, was not set to air until the fall of 2009. Waiting several months between the pilot and a second episode was an unusual strategy. "If people didn't like it, it would have been four months of negative buzz," said Joe Earley, executive vice president of marketing and communications for FOX. "We could have been killing a show before it even began."[13] However, if *Glee* could draw even a fraction of *American Idol*'s more than 27 million viewers, it would be fantastic publicity for the new show.

When the pilot aired, approximately 9.6 million viewers tuned in to watch. It was an acceptable opening, but it had lost more than 50 percent of *American Idol*'s audience. Critics had mostly

positive opinions of the show. Critic Alessandra Stanley for the *New York Times* newspaper said the show was unoriginal, but the cast was talented and appealing. Mary McNamara, a television critic for the *Los Angeles Times* was more enthusiastic: "'*Glee*' is the first show in a long time that's just plain full-throttle, no-guilty-pleasure-rationalizations-necessary fun,"[14] she wrote.

Marketing *Glee*

During the months between the May pilot and the September 9, 2009, premiere, FOX launched an intense marketing campaign to spread the word about *Glee*. "It doesn't fit neatly into a box," said FOX Broadcasting Company president Kevin Reilly. "It's comedic but it's not a comedy. It's got music but it's not a musical. And it's definitely got a little offbeat and subversive element to it, like Ryan Murphy shows do. So we thought, 'Okay, this is gonna need some word of mouth.'"[15]

To generate buzz about the show, FOX made the pilot available online over the summer. Fans could download it for free on iTunes and stream it on FOX.com and Hulu. FOX screened the show at summer camps and ran trailers with Harry Potter and the Half-Blood Prince (2009) in movie theaters. Street teams handed out *Glee*-themed merchandise to teens. Taking a page from American Idol's success, FOX released the cast's version of Journey's "Don't Stop Believin'" from the pilot on iTunes. It became an instant hit, soaring to number one on the download charts. During the summer months, FOX released more performance clips from the pilot. They did not want fans to forget *Glee* before the fall premiere.

FOX also used the young, attractive cast to promote the show. They sent cast members to Comic-Con, one of the largest conventions in the world. At Comic-Con, people can meet the casts and creators of their favorite programs. The *Glee* cast's appearance was a success, and it was accompanied by a sneak peak of *Glee*'s second episode, which delighted fans. "It was a standing-room-only crowd of several thousands of people," said Ed Martin, a television critic. "The cheering and yelling and screaming was

Lea Michele speaks with a news reporter outside of a Hot Topic store in Chicago, Illinois, during a tour to promote the show in the summer of 2009.

ear-splitting. The crowd almost blew the roof off the place with their enthusiasm for the episode."[16] After Comic-Con, cast members embarked on a ten-city mall tour. It began on August 17 in Boston, Massachusetts, where they appeared at Hot Topic clothing stores. At each stop, the cast signed autographs, held question-and-answer sessions with fans, and offered a sneak peek of the upcoming *Glee* season.

Building a Breakout Show   **19**

FOX also designed a digital strategy to promote the show. Characters had Facebook pages and Twitter accounts. The cast took handheld cameras to events and posted behind-the-scenes videos online. FOX also aired reruns of the pilot, followed by a "Tweet-peat" in which cast members and fans could discuss the episode on Twitter.

Momentum Builds

The marketing efforts paid off. FOX estimated that more than 25 million people watched *Glee*'s pilot over the summer. On September 9, 2009, when the second episode aired, 7.3 million viewers watched. After the third episode aired, FOX picked *Glee* up for a full season. The network aired thirteen episodes through December 9, 2009, and then the show took a four-month hiatus.

During the hiatus, the cast worked on the final nine episodes of the season. Cast members also traveled around the United States appearing on talk shows and giving live performances. One of the most memorable performances was at the White House, where the cast sang "Don't Stop Believin'."

The Real William McKinley High

Glee takes place at William McKinley High School, a fictional school. So that the setting appears real, the show frequently films at a real school, Juan Rodriguez Cabrillo High School, in Long Beach, California. Juan Rodriguez Cabrillo High School is no stranger to Hollywood. It has been used in films, such as Dodgeball: A True Underdog Story (2004) and Cheaper by the Dozen (2003), and in television shows, such as Bones (2005–). Some Cabrillo students were even able to join *Glee* as extras in the show's pilot episode, playing in a steel drum band.

When the show returned from its hiatus in April 2010, its audience exploded 70 percent, increasing from 7.3 million to 12.4 million viewers per episode. Passionate fans, who called themselves "*Glee*ks," loved the show's unique mix of musical theater, familiar pop tunes, and loveable underdogs. *Glee*'s momentum swept across the globe. "The international story is bloody amazing," said Rob Stringer, chairman of Columbia/Epic, *Glee*'s record label. "In Canada, the U.K., Australia, New Zealand—the *Glee* franchise is expanding, and the good news is the results are similar."[17]

Glee's Music

A huge part of the success of *Glee* is the music featured in each episode. Episodes showcase songs by famous artists, such as Neil Diamond, Rihanna, Kanye West, Barbra Streisand, Beyoncé, Queen, and Madonna. "Every single possible musical style and taste is going to be in there," said Falchuk. "It doesn't matter what you like—you're going to find what you like and stuff you never heard of that you'll love."[18] The appeal of *Glee*'s music has led to its success on the record charts. It has sold millions of albums and more than 33 million digital downloads.

Despite the popularity of the music, Brennan, Murphy, and Falchuk say that they focus on the show's story line first when creating new episodes. Then they use the music to support the story line. Falchuk says that *Glee*'s songs give viewers an emotional understanding of what the characters are feeling. "The thing about a musical is what emotional experience do you want the audience to have by hearing that song at that moment?" said Falchuk. He says that Murphy always seems to know the perfect song to fit a story line: "The songs that sell the best are the ones where the integration of the story and music really worked, where there's an emotional connection to what's going on in the scene. It's independent of genre. It could be classic rock or a musical, it's just a song that made people feel good."[19]

A touring version of Glee starring the show's cast members performs at the O2 Arena in London, England, in June 2011.

Glee on Tour

In less than a year, *Glee* became a television and music industry success. In 2010 it was announced that *Glee* was going on live tour. In May 2010 the entire cast of *Glee* went on a four-city, ten-show tour. The tour was a success, with sellout crowds in all four cities. The cast followed up on the first tour's success with a second North American tour in 2011. It also added a European tour during the summer of 2011. In only two seasons, *Glee* accomplished what many shows only dream of doing. It achieved a rare entertainment trifecta—making a lot of money in three different mediums: television, music, and live tours.

The overnight success of *Glee* amazed even Murphy, who said, "I never thought the show would even last."He explained, "I just didn't think people would get it. It truly is a show that the fans think is theirs, that they discovered it."[20] Falchuk believes that the key to the show's success is that the fans connect personally with *Glee*'s characters and the story lines. They see a part of themselves in the show's characters. "The point of the show is that every teenager is a geek," said Falchuk. "Every teenager feels a wanting, a desire for something more, to be heard, to be seen. . . . I think the show is working for people of all ages, though, because that feeling never really goes away."[21]

Chapter 2

The Lynchpin

The creators of *Glee* knew that for the show to succeed, they needed to find the right mix of actors. "Casting is always tough," said Brad Falchuk. "You're looking for what you picture in your head and put on the page, but you're looking to get surprised at the same time. We found such wonderful people, but it was a long, scary process. At times it was like, 'Are we ever going to find this person?'"[22]

Finding a Triple Threat

Falchuk and Murphy knew that the show's lynchpin would be the actor they cast to play the role of Will Schuester, the high school Spanish teacher who is in charge of the school's glee club, New Directions. He mentors and motivates his students to be the best they can be. Yet it was difficult to find a talented actor who could also sing and dance, someone who was a triple threat. When they saw Matthew Morrison, a Broadway veteran poised to make the leap to television, they knew they had found their man. "Matt's the star of the show," Murphy said. "The show rests on his shoulders—everything revolves around him."[23]

Born in Fort Ord, California, Morrison was a quiet, shy child. "I grew up as an only child," he said. "My parents weren't great conversationalists. We had a quiet house. I'm not very verbal."[24] Morrison credits the hours he spent alone with helping him develop his acting skills. "My mom was an RN [registered nurse] and my dad was a midwife [a person who helps women during childbirth], and they were working all the time. I had this wild imagination, and I'd come home after school and stage these whole scenes with my toy knights,"[25] he said.

Morrison became interested in acting when he was ten years old and spending the summer with family in Arizona, where he attended a children's theater camp. Onstage, Morrison finally felt comfortable. "I was really lucky when I stumbled into theater. It felt great living in someone else's skin."[26] he said.

As a teenager, Morrison auditioned and won a place at the prestigious Orange County High School of the Arts (OCHSA). He split his time between regular school and OCHSA. "I did all my academics and then from 2 p.m. to 6 p.m., I went to a performing-arts high school. I loved it,"[27] he said. Morrison remembers his high school years fondly. "All the kids in the cast [of *Glee*] tell me they hated high school, but I had the best time," he said. "I guess I was one of the popular kids. I played soccer, I was class president—I even dated the homecoming queen."[28]

Morrison played soccer so well that he considered training full-time for the U.S. national team and a chance to play in the Olympics. Yet pursuing soccer on that level requires a significant time commitment, and Morrison would have had to give up performing and theater. After careful consideration and soul-searching, he made the hard decision to focus his talents on performing arts.

Morrison Moves to New York City

After graduating from OCHSA in 1997, Morrison headed east to New York University's esteemed Tisch School of the Arts. At Tisch, Morrison studied musical theater, vocal performance, and dance. He believes that if he had not gone to New York City, then his life might have been a lot like Mr. Schuester's. "I feel like if I hadn't gone to New York, [I] would have gone to [California State University Chico] in Northern California, and I probably would have done theater, come back to Southern California and taught at a performing arts high school. That would have been my path,"[29] he said.

Matthew Morrison arrives at the after-party following the opening night of Hairspray *on Broadway in August 2002.*

Morrison's hard work paid off, and within two years he got an agent and his first small roles on Broadway. In 1998 Morrison played Chuck Cranston, an abusive boyfriend, in *Footloose*. In 2002, he joined *The Rocky Horror Picture Show* as one of the masked phantoms.

Also in 2002, Morrison won the role of Link Larkin in the original production of *Hairspray*. His portrayal of the teen heartthrob earned him respect in the theater community and more work. In 2005, Morrison was nominated for a Tony Award, one of Broadway's highest honors, for his leading role in *The Light in the Piazza*. He also starred in the Tony Award–winning revival of *South Pacific* at the Lincoln Center Theater in 2008.

While working on Broadway, Morrison also explored other areas of performing. He joined the boy band LMNT (pronounced "Element") in 2001. He quickly discovered that he hated the experience and quit before the band released its first album. In 2006, Morrison appeared on the popular television soap opera *As the World Turns* (1956–2010). Working on a soap opera, however, meant learning scripts on a daily basis, and Morrison did not enjoy the work. He also had several small roles and guest spots on *Sex and the City* (1998–2004), *Law & Order: Criminal Intent*

The Lynchpin **25**

History of Glee Clubs

So what is a glee club? Historically, it was a musical or choral group that sang short songs called glees in groups of three or four singers without music. The first named glee club was formed in 1787 at the Harrow School in London, England. Traditionally, glee clubs were primarily male voices, but later singers formed all-female or mixed-voice groups.

By the nineteenth century, glee clubs became popular in many schools, with most schools forming their own club. In the United States, the oldest glee club is the Harvard Glee Club, founded in 1858 at Harvard University in Cambridge, Massachusetts. The club initially consisted of a dozen or two men who sang a variety of songs including college and folk songs, contemporary art songs, and popular operetta and show tunes. The Harvard Glee Club performed at home as well as throughout the Northeast. Other universities quickly followed Harvard's lead and formed their own glee clubs, including the University of Michigan in 1859, Yale in 1861, and Cornell in 1868.

Show choirs, which combine choral singing with dancing, emerged in the 1960s. The Young Americans and Up with People were two of the first show choirs. When students and teachers saw these groups, it inspired them to start similar show choirs in their schools. In the 1970s and 1980s, show choirs exploded in popularity, especially in California and the midwestern states.

The Harvard Glee Club, shown here in the 1870s but founded in 1858, is the oldest one of its kind in the United States.

26 The Creators and Cast of *Glee*

(2001–2011), *CSI: Miami* (2002–), and *Numb3rs* (2005–2010), and he traveled to Los Angeles several times to shoot television pilots, but none of them were picked up by the networks.. Morrison also appeared in small roles in films, such as *Dan in Real Life* (2007) and *Music and Lyrics* (2007).

Morrison Auditions for *Glee*

Then Morrison auditioned for *Glee*. Dozens of actors read for the role of Mr. Schuester, but according to Murphy, they lacked the empathy needed for the glee club director. When Morrison auditioned, he chose not to belt out a standard Broadway tune like other actors did. Instead, he sang a low-key version of "Somewhere over the Rainbow" and played his ukulele. Almost immediately, Murphy knew that he had found Will Schuester. Even though Morrison won the role, he was cautious. He was not convinced that *Glee* would be accepted by network executives and viewers. "I didn't really think this was the one that was going to make it,"[30] Morrison said.

Regardless of his expectations, Morrison admitted that the role of Will Schuester was a perfect fit. "If I could have written a part for myself, this would have been it," he said. "It showcases everything I've trained for, and it's the kind of teaching job I could easily have wound up doing myself in real life."[31] His fellow cast members noticed the similarity between nice guy Mr. Schuester and Morrison. "[He] really sets the tone for the cast and the crew. (He's) so focused and always ready to work and just so generous with his time. He's happy to run lines (with other actors) the whole time between shots,"[32] said Jayma Mays, who plays Emma Pillsbury, the school guidance counselor who is in love with Mr. Schuesters. Jane Lynch, who plays the scheming cheerleading coach Sue Sylvester, agrees with Mays. "[Morrison is] good-hearted and extremely compassionate. Any time I get petty or gossipy around him, I always feel bad because he's not that guy,"[33] she said.

Even though he shares characteristics with his character, Morrison points out one major difference between himself and

Morrison's role as Spanish teacher and glee club director, Mr. Schuester, allows him to showcase his acting, singing, and dancing skills.

Mr. Schuester: "After high school, he [Schuester] never really had the confidence and courage to go after his dream. . . . I knew what I wanted."[34]

Ups and Downs of Stardom

Although Morrison had doubts, fans worldwide enthusiastically embraced *Glee*, and the show's wild success rocketed Morrison and the rest of the cast into stardom. "This is certainly the most recognized I've ever been in my life. . . . More people saw the pilot of *Glee* than saw me in my entire 10-year career on Broadway. But people feel more of a connection to you because they see you in their living rooms,"[35] he said.

Morrison admits that fame has its drawbacks. Being recognized wherever he goes is unsettling for the actor, who treasures his anonymity. "You know, none of us have experienced this kind of notoriety before," Morrison said. "But we've [the cast of *Glee*] gone through it as a family and we keep each other grounded and in check."[36] Another drawback of fame is the additional pressure actors feel. "It's a tough thing," Morrison said. "I really enjoyed the struggle of being an actor. There's something about having big dreams and going after them. Once you reach a certain kind of success there's a toll to maintain that success; and there's a lot more expectations. It's hard."[37]

To escape the demands of fame and Hollywood, Morrison spends time golfing, running, boxing, skydiving, and cycling. He also tried new projects and released his first solo record album in 2011. The self-titled album features duets with music icons Elton John and Sting.

In the future Morrison hopes to build upon his success with *Glee*. "I hope to be one of those guys who has a strong presence in every genre of the entertainment world. I've kind of established myself on Broadway and on TV with *Glee*, and I'd eventually like to do some film work. I want to do it all,"[38] he said.

Mr. Schuester's Wife

Mr. Schuester is married, and his wife, Terri, was his high school sweetheart. Terri is played by Canadian actress Jessalyn Gilsig.

Born in Montreal, Gilsig attended the Trafalgar School for Girls, where she studied theater and arts. She then earned an English degree from Montreal's McGill University before honing her acting skills at the American Repertory Theater at Harvard University in Cambridge, Massachusetts. There she appeared in several productions, including *The Cherry Orchard, Henry V, The Oresteia, Tartuffe,* and the *Tempest.*

In 1995, Gilsig moved to New York City and starred in several off-Broadway shows. She also landed guest star roles on several television series, including *Viper* (1994) and *Seven Days* (1998–2001). Her big break came when television producer David E. Kelley cast her in a guest role on the hit drama *The Practice* (1997–2004). Gilsig appeared in only two episodes, but Kelley was impressed with her work. He wrote the part of Lauren Davis on his next show, *Boston Public* (2000–2004), specifically for Gilsig. The series premiered in October 2000.

After two years on *Boston Public,* Gilsig left the show in 2002. Next she signed on with *Nip/Tuck* in 2003, playing the role of Gina Russo. She stayed with the show until her character was killed off in 2008. Over the next few years, she appeared in recurring roles on several hit television shows, including *NYPD Blue* (1994–2005), *Prison Break* (2005–2009), *Law & Order* (1990–2010), *Friday Night Lights* (2006–2011), and *Heroes* (2006–2010). Gilsig also experimented with film roles, landing small parts in movies, such as *The Stepfather* (2009) and *Prom Night* (2008).

Gilsig Joins *Glee*

Gilsig's work on Murphy's *Nip/Tuck* helped her win a role on *Glee*. Murphy admits that he wrote the role of Terri Schuester with Gilsig in mind. When he approached Gilsig with the idea, she was thrilled with the chance to work with Murphy again. She said working on *Nip/Tuck*

> was one of the best experiences as an actor I've ever had in my career.... And for me, the opportunity to do a comedy is something that I've been itching to do for many years now and also if I was going to do that—which is kind of a big risk for me—to be able to do that with Ryan, who I know so well, and then so much of the crew that I was familiar with from *Nip/Tuck* was kind of a dream scenario.[39]

Terri Schuester has become the woman *Glee* fans love to hate. "She so identifies with high school when she was her very best that she really hasn't evolved out of that place. I mean, her hair.... She has like 1988 cheerleader hair!" Gilsig said. "Terri just needs

Jessalyn Gilsig has said that she thinks it's fun to play the unlikable Terri Schuester, Mr. Schuester's wife.

to step into the now and let go of the past."[40] Gilsig believes that the core of Terri's problems is an intense lack of self-confidence. "As we go on, we realize that her motivation is this incredibly deep insecurity that if [her husband] really knew who she was, then he wouldn't stay with her," she said. "I feel like that's very human."[41]

Although it can be difficult playing a character disliked by so

The Lynchpin 31

many, Gilsig enjoys the challenge. "I think there are just a lot of people who think she's a nut job, basically. Which I guess she is. But it's fun to play those parts. You kind of want to be the person who stirs up controversy. It keeps the show interesting I think,"[42] she said.

Show Choirs in the Twenty-First Century

In the early twenty-first century show choirs were popular in high schools across the United States, especially in California and the Midwest. Many students were involved in the choirs, in different ways. Most choirs had between thirty and sixty performers, a band, and a technical team. Most choirs required prospective performers to audition, and some also required a membership fee that helped pay for the choir's expenses.

Financing a show choir is expensive. Choirs need to budget for costumes, props, travel expenses, and music-licensing fees. Some choirs also hire vocal coaches and choreographers to help them polish their performances.

Most show choirs perform sets that include a variety of songs. There may be several fast-tempo, choreographed numbers and at least one slower piece with little choreography, that highlights the group's singing talent. Unlike *Glee*, where the students seem to learn new routines in a matter of days or even hours, a real-life show choir needs months to learn and perfect a new musical routine. Choirs may practice during or after school hours. In addition to working on their vocals, most of the performers train in dance, so that they can incorporate a variety of styles from classical to hip-hop into their routines.

Many show choirs compete in competitions called invitationals. They can be as small as a few groups or may include many choirs from several states. In some of the larger competitions, the choirs are divided into divisions by age, skill level, school size, or gender. Some prestigious national competitions draw choirs from across the United States and take place in large venues with professional lighting and sound.

The Counselor Who Loves Mr. Schuester

Many *Glee* fans are rooting for another woman in Will Schuester's life, quirky school guidance counselor Emma Pillsbury. Played by actress Jayma Mays, Emma is also in love with Will.

Growing up as the youngest of three children in small-town Grundy, Virginia, Mays had an active imagination. She loved dressing up in costumes and pretending to be different characters. Yet it was not until high school that Mays realized her love of performing. "We had a program called forensics [in high school].... It was kind of an extracurricular activity. You'd perform monologues after school and compete against other teams. That was my first real taste of performing in front of people, and I loved it. So, when I went to college after a couple years I took some classes and was just completely hooked,"[43] she said.

After graduating from Radford University with a degree in performing arts, Mays moved to Los Angeles. She said,

> The bulk of work in film and television is out here, and I think I knew that was

Jayma Mays appeared in several television shows and movies before landing the role of guidance counselor Emma Pillsbury.

how I wanted to make my career. I moved out to L.A. and started working really hard [sending out headshots and doing theater performances] . . . before someone saw me in one of the theater shows and had me come in and audition for a small part on Matt LeBlanc's television show *Joey*. From there, I got a really great manager and started getting more and more roles in television.[44]

Mays had recurring roles on the hit television series *Ugly Betty* (2006–2010) and *Heroes*. She also appeared in films, including *Epic Movie* (2007) and *Paul Blart: Mall Cop* (2009). In 2009, Mays joined the cast of *Glee*. As soon as she read the script, Mays knew that she wanted to be a part of the show. "The second I read it I thought, 'Gosh, if I could be a part of this project it would be fantastic.' It had everything going for it. It's different, quirky, it's a fight for the underdog and it's got music in it. Everything about it made it a no-brainer situation,"[45] she said.

According to Mays, Emma is an interesting character. She is practical, with a fear of germs and a little bit of obsessive-compulsive disorder. She is also a romantic at heart, falling for Will even though he is a married man. "I think the challenge comes from Emma just having many layers built in to her with her being manic and I feel like she's always afraid of something in the room because there are rooms everywhere. Then, you add into that the fact she's lusting after a married man. I always feel like there are a lot of things going on with her, but that's what makes her so wonderful to play, too,"[46] she said.

In one way, Mays admits that Emma is rubbing off on her: "After we [the show] got picked up and we started filming the first few episodes, I kind of started getting that feeling of needing to wash my hands all the time. And I started keeping antibacterial stuff in my purse."[47]

Mays has been surprised by the phenomenal success of *Glee*. "We all kind of knew that there was something special about the show because it was different and the writing was exciting. . . . I don't think we had any idea that people would gravitate towards it like they have. That's been a real shock and a real surprise and a bit overwhelming but just absolutely wonderful,"[48] she said.

Chapter 3

The Driving Force

While Will Schuester is the lynchpin of *Glee*, ambitious and energetic Rachel Berry is its driving force. Played by actress Lea Michele, confident Rachel is often insufferable in her drive to shine on stage. "Rachel is very much like me when I was about 10 to 12, working in theater, very driven.... I understand her. I was similar in the sense that I didn't conform to what people thought was cool. It was important to do what I believed in,"[49] said Michele.

Lea Michele Sarfati was born in New York to an Italian American mom and a Spanish father. She later moved to Tenafly, New Jersey, where she attended and graduated from Tenafly High School. Around the age of eight, Michele went to see *Phantom of the Opera* on Broadway with a friend's family. "I remember not knowing what Broadway was, or what it meant. I remember sitting on the edge of my seat and thinking, 'Oh my God, this is amazing.' I got the CD and took it home and learned all the words,"[50] she said.

Broadway Beginnings

A short time later, there was an open casting call for the role of young Cosette in the stage production of *Les Miserables*. Michele's friend wanted to audition, but her father had fallen ill and was unable to drive her. When Michele's mom volunteered to drive, Michele spontaneously decided to audition as well. "I didn't know I could sing until I auditioned for *Les Miserables*. My friend was

35

Lea Michele, performing one of Glee's production numbers, began her career as a child with a part in Les Miserables on Broadway.

auditioning, and I wanted to audition too. My mother was like, 'You can't sing.' I'd never tried!" she said. But Michele had been listening to the *Phantom* CD and sang "Angel of Music" a cappella in her audition. "After the audition, I said, 'Mom, I think they really like me.' She said if we ever hear from them again, it will be a miracle,"[51] Michele recalled.

Michele got the part, and a few weeks later, she debuted on Broadway as Young Cosette. Her performance led to her next part as the Little Girl with the original cast of *Ragtime* in Toronto, Ontario, Canada, in 1998. Michele and her mom moved to Canada so that she could do the show, while her father stayed behind to run the family deli. The show later moved to Broadway, with Michele. In 1998, the show received twelve Tony Award nominations, including best musical.

Growing with *Spring Awakenings*

At the age of fourteen, Michele auditioned for and won the role of Wendla Bergman in the workshop production of *Spring Awakening*, an adaptation of an 1891 play by Frank Wedekind. The play, which addressed the issues of masturbation, sexual exploration, rape, pregnancy, and abortion, was controversial. Michele loved the complicated role of Wendla, whose inexperience leads her to become pregnant and eventually die from an abortion. While working in the show Michele was able to fit in a few years of high school life. "While I did workshops of *Spring Awakening* during my freshman, sophomore, and junior years of high school I wasn't really auditioning very much because I wanted to give myself time to focus on school and I wanted to just have a normal high school life for a little while,"[52] she said.

Michele admits that she was not one of the popular kids in high school. "I wasn't the coolest kid, but I got by. I played volleyball, I was a varsity debater—I won a lot of trophies for that; I talk very fast!—and I only did one play and one musical because I wanted to give other people an opportunity. I also had a long-term high school boyfriend . . . and a nice group of friends. It was really normal,"[53] she said. Still, her time in high school made her even more certain that she wanted to become an actor.

Decision Time

At the end of high school, Michele faced a crossroads. She had been accepted into the Tisch School of the Arts at New York University. She had also landed a role in her third Broadway show,

Jonathan Groff

Actor Jonathan Groff plays Jesse St. James on *Glee*. He had a couple of connections to the show before he even joined the cast during the second half of the first season. He is real-life best friends with Lea Michele, who plays Rachel Berry. They met while starring together in *Spring Awakening* on Broadway in 2006. *Spring Awakening* was Groff's first big Broadway role, and he earned a Tony Award nomination for his performance. Groff also knew *Glee* creator Ryan Murphy prior to joining the cast. In 2008 Groff had a role in the television pilot for *Pretty/Handsome*, a show created by Murphy, who directed the pilot. The show was not selected to become a regular series.

With these connections to *Glee*, it was only a matter of time before Groff joined the show. Murphy was so impressed with Groff's work on *Pretty/Handsome*, he promised the actor that he would write a part for him in *Glee*. That part is Jesse St. James, a male diva from Vocal Adrenaline, a rival high school's show choir. As St. James, Groff has been able to showcase his amazing voice and add a new level of drama to the show.

Fiddler on the Roof. If she attended Tisch, she would have to turn down the *Fiddler* role. Michele recalled,

> When *Fiddler* came it was a big deciding point in my life. I had just been accepted into NYU, and I was just about to graduate and to head to college so it was a real deciding factor for me—which way is your life going to go? The college route and act a little bit on the side and major in law or something or are you just going to really give yourself to this? And that's what I decided to do. When I graduated I got an apartment in the city and I decided to not go to NYU and I've been working from then on.[54]

Even after Michele chose to continue on Broadway, she faced

more tough choices. She had stayed with *Spring Awakening* throughout the workshop process, but when it was finally about to open on Broadway, Michele was offered the plum role of Eponine in *Les Miserables*. In the end, Michele could not turn her back on Wendla and *Spring Awakening*. She chose to stay with the production.

In hindsight, the decision was a great one. The show opened to critical acclaim in December 2006. It was nominated for eleven Tony Awards in 2007 and won eight. Also in 2007 Michele received a nomination for a Drama Desk Award for Outstanding Actress in a Musical for her performance.

Michele credits *Spring Awakening* for her development as an actress and singer:

Lea Michele joins fellow Spring Awakening cast members, John Gallagher Jr., left, and Jonathan Groff, to introduce their performance at the 2007 Tony Awards.

The Driving Force **39**

I did every conception, every workshop of that show from when I was 14 years old. I brought it to Off-Broadway, then Broadway. It's a rare thing that starting at such a young age, someone would continue in a project for so long. Generally, kids will outgrow the part, or they'll want to try someone new. But I really grew into this role; my voice grew a lot. I started off as a quiet soprano, but over the years, my voice opened up to a legit belter, kind of. That really helped me . . . as I got older, I was able to deal with the weight of Spring Awakening. It's a very dark play. As I got older, I could deal with those issues, and I think they felt more comfortable as the years went on in taking it a bit further.[55]

By coincidence, *Spring Awakening* also led to Michele being cast in the role of Rachel Berry. Her costar and best friend, Jonathan Groff, flew out to Los Angeles in 2007 to shoot a television pilot for Ryan Murphy. At the time, the Broadway stagehands were on strike, and the Eugene O'Neill theater, where Michele performed, was shut down. Instead of sitting at home, she decided to visit Groff in California. During her visit, Michele had dinner with Groff and Murphy. Unknown to her, she made a lasting impression on the *Glee* creator.

Auditioning for *Glee*

After two years on Broadway, Michele left *Spring Awakening* and moved to Los Angeles. "I came out to L.A. because I was cast as Eponine in *Les Mis* at the Hollywood Bowl—something like a four-to-six week engagement. I figured I'd come out and try L.A. for a month or two after that, try out for some pilots or some guest spots for TV shows. *Glee* was the second audition that I went on,"[56] she said.

Actually, Michele almost missed her *Glee* audition. On the way to the FOX studio in Los Angeles, she got into a car accident. Instead of missing the audition, however, Michele abandoned her totaled car on the side of the road and walked the rest of the way. "I literally had chunks of glass that I pulled from my hair and put

Michele's role as perfectionist Rachel Berry was written with her in mind.

The Driving Force 41

on the table. I look back on that day and think, I can't believe I did that. I left the car on the side of the road. But something came over me,"[57] she said.

Michele sang "On My Own" from *Les Miserables* and nailed the audition. After she was cast as Rachel Berry, Murphy admitted that he had written the role for her. "It was written for her. We had the prototype, which was a Reese Witherspoon *Election*-esque Broadway baby [actress Witherspoon played a student in the 1999 movie *Election*] that was a mix of [singing legends] Barbra Streisand and Patti LuPone," Murphy said. "I really believed in Michele's talent because her talent was once in a lifetime."[58] Michele, however, did not know that during the audition. "I wish I'd known; I would have been less nervous," she said. "I didn't think I'd ever be as lucky to find a part that's so right for me."[59]

Rachel Berry

Rachel Berry is a perfectionist. She was adopted and raised by two gay dads and wants to be the star singer of the glee club, New Directions, at William McKinley High School. Rachel's ambition drives her to join the club, hoping it will be her ticket to stardom. Her character is complex, especially when her drive to be the best is at odds with her desire to be liked by her peers. The show highlights Rachel's struggles with acceptance, friendship, and first loves.

Michele and Rachel share similar qualities. "[Michele is] very ambitious and driven, and she's got her eye on the prize. She's always been focused," Murphy said. "Talking to her mother, she's been that way from birth."[60] Michele and Rachel also share a love of singing and performing, which is how Michele really shines on the show. For this, Michele's theater training is useful in helping her play the over-the-top, energetic Rachel.

With dark hair and eyes, Michele knows that she does not physically fit the Hollywood actress stereotype, and she embraces her looks and hopes to become a role model for girls. "I love me and my body and my Jewish nose. If that is inspiring and can give young girls a sense of confidence, that's great."[61]

42 The Creators and Cast of *Glee*

Piano Man Brad Ellis

Brad Ellis is the man who plays the piano for the students in *Glee*. He is a real musician, not an actor. Ellis trained at the Berklee College of Music in Boston, Massachusetts. Then he spent several years working on off-Broadway productions, such as *Forbidden Broadway*. In 2006, he arranged music for singer-pianist Billy Joel's Waltz Variations no.2 op. 5. He also composed music for the 2009 Broadway musical *The Tin Pan Alley Rag*.

Ellis was originally hired by *Glee* to accompany hopeful actors during auditions for the show. He worked so well with the singers that Ryan Murphy casually mentioned one day that Ellis should be in the show and play piano for the singers. At first Ellis thought that Murphy was joking, but the idea took hold and soon Ellis was dressed in black, filming episodes with the cast.

Brad Ellis, right, is the piano player who accompanies the singers in New Directions.

The Driving Force

Working on Set

When shooting episodes of *Glee*, Michele and the rest of the cast usually work twelve to fourteen hours each day. Michele reports to hair and make-up at 6 A.M.. Then she shoots scenes with the other actors or rehearses choreography in the dance studio. Michele and the other cast members also have to learn production numbers for *Glee*'s national tours.

Her cast mates say that Michele thrives on the hard work. "She always has everything down before she comes to set, her lines and her songs. She's a perfectionist in every way. She walks around with her notebook and makes her to-do lists,"[62] says Jenna Ushkowitz, who plays fellow glee club member Tina Cohen-Chang.

Michele has received recognition for her hard work. In 2009 she was nominated for a Teen Choice Award for Choice TV Breakout Star, and she won the Satellite Award for Best Actress in a Series. In 2010 she was nominated for a Golden Globe Award for Best Actress in a TV Series, Comedy or Musical. Although she did not win, Michele was still amazed with the nomination. "When I found out I was nominated for a Golden Globe in the category that I was nominated in, I was in complete shock. . . . It is such an

Michele arrives at the 2011 Emmy Awards, at which she was nominated for Outstanding Lead Actress in a Comedy Series.

honor, something I never thought I would be lucky enough to have happen to me in my life. I feel so truly blessed and thankful,"[63] she said.

In 2011 Michele was again nominated for a Golden Globe Award and Teen Choice Award for her performance as Rachel Berry. She also received a nomination for the Emmy Award for Outstanding Lead Actress in a Comedy Series. *Time* magazine placed her on its 2010 list of the 100 Most Influential People in the World.

A Shiny Future

Looking toward the future, Michele has numerous opportunities in front of her. Michele's character on *Glee* is scheduled to graduate at the end of the third season, along with fellow seniors Finn and Kurt. "We always knew we'd graduate in real time. It's all part of the plan and it's all good! It's going to make Season 3 amazing!!!"[64] Michele tweeted to fans. Producers have been tight-lipped about how the trio will be included in the show's story line going forward.

Regardless, Michele's star has never been brighter. Her singing is a prominently featured on the show, during live tours, and on *Glee* soundtracks. It is no surprise that Columbia Records signed Michele to record her own solo album. Michele is also breaking in to the movies. She landed a role in the 2011 film *New Year's Eve*, directed by Garry Marshall and costarring Sarah Jessica Parker, Jessica Biel, and Ashton Kutcher. She also joined the cast of the animated film *Dorothy of Oz,* in which she will be the voice of the lead role of Dorothy Gale. The film is scheduled for release in late 2012.

No matter what the future holds, Michele plans to attack it with a Rachel Berry–like determination. "I don't stop," Michele says. "It's my nature. People have to tell me to slow down. I plan on playing every role on Broadway. . . . I want to do movies, make music. *Glee* is only the beginning."[65]

Chapter 4

The *Glee* Club

When Mr. Schuester takes over the struggling glee club, New Directions, in the first episode of *Glee*, only four students are willing members alongside the indomitable Rachel Berry: school misfits Mercedes Jones, Kurt Hummel, Artie Abrams, and Tina Cohen-Chang. These four core members of the club provide much of the heart of *Glee*.

Mercedes Jones

Glee producers had a hard time finding the right actress for the part of Mercedes Jones, the diva with a huge voice. They needed a singer with an amazingly powerful voice, someone with enough rhythm to dance and who could bring Mercedes' complex character to life on-screen. "We couldn't find her anywhere," said casting director Robert Ulrich. "One day, a friend said, 'My roommate's friend sings.' . . . So I said, 'Have her come in.'"[66] The roommate's friend was Amber Riley, and she was just right.

When Riley was about two years old, her mother noticed her musical talent and began training her daughter. Riley had her first performance in a local park, when she was only four years old. As a teenager, Riley knew that she wanted to perform and worked hard to make her dream come true. She sang background and performed with the Los Angeles Opera in productions like *Alice in Wonderland, A Midsummer Night's Dream, Mystery on the Docks,* and *Into the Woods*. She did not, however, sing in a high school glee club. "We didn't have a glee club in school. I kind of

Amber Riley was a stage and television actress and auditioned for American Idol before landing the role of Mercedes Jones.

The Glee Club   **47**

wish we did because if I was back in high school now, I definitely would join!"[67] she said.

In 2002 Riley was cast in a television pilot called *St. Sass.* Unfortunately, the show was not picked up by a network. But one of the pilot's writers, Ryan Murphy, would become an important connection later in Riley's career. Based on her work on *St. Sass,* Riley landed a role in the *Cedric the Entertainer Presents* (2002–2003) comedy show in 2002. Although she did not get to show off her big voice, Riley did not mind. She said, "I've always loved singing and acting equally and I was like, 'Well whichever one takes off first, I'm sure the other one will follow!'"[68]

For the next few years, Riley auditioned for a variety of roles. She remembers that although producers and casting agents praised her, they did not call to offer her the part. "The feedback was, 'You're a great singer! You're a great actress!' And then I don't get the call," said Riley. Instead, Riley said that she was told, "I was a little big for the role or 'She's not the look we want.'"[69] Although Riley knew that she did not look like a typical Hollywood starlet, she refused to let it stop her from trying to achieve her dream of performing. "I could tell it would be hard for me to break into the business because of what the Hollywood standard is," said Riley. "My voice and my gift gave me confidence."[70]

In 2005 Riley auditioned for *American Idol.* The show's producers passed over the teen, not even giving her the chance to sing in front of the show's celebrity judges. Yet Riley refused to let the rejection stop her from reaching for her dreams. "My life was crushed when they [*American Idol*] told me 'No', but I was 17, it was a long time ago and rejection like that only makes you stronger, gets you asking—how can I better myself?"[71] she said.

When Riley arrived for her *Glee* audition in 2008, she actually thought that she was auditioning for a background singing gig. The producers asked her to sing "And I Am Telling You I'm Not Going" from *Dreamgirls,* which was a play that was later made into a movie (2006) starring Eddie Murphy, Jamie Foxx, Beyoncé, and Jennifer Hudson. Riley had never sung the song before, but she sealed the audition with her rendition. Within two weeks, she had the part. "Everything happened so fast and I'm blessed to be a part of something so influential to young people and to be having so much fun living a part of my dream!"[72] she said.

Like many people, Riley was surprised at how well and how fast *Glee* achieved success. She attributes the show's success to its musical roots. "I think that people really like the music—everyone responds to music so well. There's so many different types of music that we sing on the show—so many genres—and also some people see their own high school experiences through characters on the show,"[73] she said.

For Riley, starring on *Glee* opened many doors and led to experiences that she could only dream of in the past. "In high school, I had to write a bucket list. Meeting the president, being on *Oprah*, and going to—not being nominated for —the Grammys were on my list. And I've done all of that through *Glee*,"[74] she said.

Kurt Hummel

Glee producers created the character of Kurt Hummel for Chris Colfer, because the actor had impressed them so much during his audition for the show. They named the new character Kurt because Colfer had once played Kurt Von Trapp in *The Sound of Music*. They chose the last name Hummel because Murphy thought that Colfer looked like the popular rosy-cheeked porcelain figurines called Hummels.

Colfer's first role was as Snoopy in a school play when he was eight years old. His mother, Karyn Colfer, remembers how being onstage made him shine. "We had this child, Christopher, who was extremely gifted in all areas. He was very smart academically. He was very mature for his age. . . . And this was his outlet. It was a way for him to have something that was his very own, and his father and I were committed to making sure that he went after this,"[75] she said. With his parents' support, Colfer performed in local plays several nights a week between the ages of nine and fourteen.

In high school, Colfer excelled at performing and the creative arts. He was a speech and debate champion and president of the writer's club. He also wrote and performed a spoof of the musical *Sweeney Todd* that he called "Shirley Todd." Still, Colfer admits

The Glee Club **49**

that his time in high school was not easy. He rarely went out with friends, instead preferring to stay home and write or help take care of his younger sister, Hannah, who was born with a critical illness. In addition Colfer's uniquely high-pitched voice often attracted unwanted attention. "I was made fun of a lot in high school because of the way I sound and the way I was. I was a lone duck in a swan-filled pond who criticized everyone,"[76] he said.

It was not long before Colfer got a Hollywood agent, and his

Mike O'Malley

Actor Mike O'Malley sensitively portrays Burt Hummel, Kurt Hummel's father, in *Glee*. In a memorable episode in the first season, Kurt finally finds the courage to tell his father that he is gay, and Burt surprises his son with his support. Before he accepted the role of Hummel, O'Malley appeared in a number of movies, including *Deep Impact* (1998), *Pushing Tin* (1999), and *28 Days* (2000), and starred in the television show, *Yes, Dear* (2000–2006). He is also an accomplished playwright. Two of his plays, *Three Years from Thirty* and *Diverting Devotion* have been produced off Broadway.

Veteran character actor Mike O'Malley plays Kurt Hummel's father, Burt.

Chris Colfer, singing a number from the live Glee touring show, developed his love of performing as a child.

mother began driving him eight hours round-trip from their home in Clovis, California, to auditions in Los Angeles. He tried out for about thirty roles, without much success. "I'm horrible at auditions anyway. Maybe that's why I never got anything,"[77] Colfer admitted.

Then the soft-spoken eighteen-year-old tried out for *Glee*. At first, Colfer read for the part of Artie Abrams. He sang "Mr. Cellophane" from the musical *Chicago*, which he had rehearsed

The character of Kurt Hammel was written for Colfer after he originally auditioned for the part of Artie Abrams.

with his grandmother. The producers saw that Colfer was not the right actor for the role of Artie, but they recognized that he had something special. "He was unique," said Ulrich. "He had such an unusual sound that we immediately loved him. We took him to Ryan and said, 'This kid might not be right for any part, but he's too special for you not to see him.'"[78]

Murphy and the other producers decided to add another character to the show, one that would fit Colfer perfectly. "I got a call from my agent saying that they didn't want me for Artie but they wanted me for this new character they were writing. . . . I went through the network auditions and the studio auditions and I got a call later from my agent, who said that I got the role and that the role had actually been written for me,"[79] said Colfer.

The character that the producers created was Kurt Hummel, a gay teenager, based on Murphy's experiences growing up as a gay youth in Indiana. "When we started auditioning, I thought it was kind of ridiculous that we're doing a musical about kids and expression and we don't have the gay point of view. I thought it was important, but I would never want Chris to feel weird. More than the gay thing, he understood the thing about being an outsider because he felt that way in high school and I told him we're going to tap into that,"[80] Murphy said.

By playing a gay character and coming out as gay himself, Colfer hopes to help other gay youths. "I think it's extremely important for gay youth out there to see that it's actually OK and that they are being represented in these shows,"[81] he said.

Jumping into the role of Kurt was exhilarating and challenging for Colfer. A novice, with no formal acting, singing, or dance training, Colfer found himself in a show that featured music and dance productions in every episode. "Dancing is the one thing I really came to *Glee* with very little experience in. . . . That's been the biggest education to me, learning how to dance and learning how my body moves,"[82] Colfer said.

Despite his inexperience, Colfer seems to be making all the right moves. His sensitive portrayal of Kurt has the made the character one of the most loved by fans. He was also nominated for several awards, winning a Golden Globe Award in 2011. Colfer also received an Emmy Award nomination for his performace in 2011. In reaction to Colfer's performance in an antibullying story line in the second season, *Time* named Colfer to its 2011 Time 100, the magazine's list of the most influential people in the world.

Playing Kurt on *Glee* opened many doors for Colfer. He signed a deal with Disney to write a live-action pilot for a children's show

Darren Criss

Actor Darren Criss joined the cast of *Glee* in the second season as Blaine Anderson, a student at the all-male Dalton Academy and leader of their glee club, the Warblers. Show creator Ryan Murphy added Blaine to be a love interest for Kurt Hummel, a gay character.

Criss grew up in San Francisco and learned to play a variety of instruments, including the violin, guitar, piano, and drums at a young age. He played drums in a small band with his brother, before leaving to attend the University of Michigan and study acting.

In his senior year of college, Criss attracted the attention of millions of people when he and some friends created an online video called, *A Very Potter Musical*. The musical comedy, based on J.K. Rowling's Harry Potter series, became a YouTube sensation and provided a platform for Criss and his partners to form StarKid Productions. Within a year, they had written and produced more online hits, including *A Very Potter Sequel* and gathered a worldwide following. Criss also appeared on television in *Eastwick* (2009) and *Cold Case* (2003–2010).

As Blaine on *Glee*, Criss delivered a breakout performance when he sang "Teenage Dream" in his first episode. The song, from an album of the same name by singer Katy Perry, was already popular, and Criss's version set a record for *Glee*. It debuted at number one on the Billboard charts and sold more than two hundred thousand tracks in its first week.

---

called "The Little Leftover Witch" for the Disney Channel. In the summer of 2011, Colfer filmed *Struck by Lightning*, a movie based on a screenplay he wrote. It is scheduled to be released in 2012. He has also hard at work writing a book series for children for which he already has a publisher.

On *Glee*'s success, Colfer says, "I think there are so many things for people to relate to—there's either a character or a situation that people can identify with and then we add music to that. Music is a universal language and when you add that to the mix—I mean, it's unstoppable."[83]

Artie Abrams

Paralyzed from the waist down after a car accident when he was a child, Artie Abrams is in a wheelchair. Learning to move and dance in a wheelchair presented a unique challenge for able-bodied actor Kevin McHale. "You know, it took a little getting used to. But that's the part, I never thought twice about it. It was just, 'How am I going to make this as believable and as good as possible.' Getting used to and memorizing choreography in a wheelchair as opposed to standing up, that's definitely a different mindset, but I like it,"[84] said McHale.

Getting the part of Artie was McHale's big break into show business. McHale had previously appeared in small parts in episodes of *The Office* (2005–), *Zoey 101* (2005), and *True Blood* (2008), and he

Kevin McHale acted in several small television parts and performed as part of a boy band before joining the cast of Glee as Artie Abrams.

spent about six years, from 2003 to 2009, in a boy band called NLT (Not Like Them). The band released four singles between March 2007 and April 2008 but never released a full album. "We had a few singles out. We did OK. Then one of the guys left the group and wanted to go solo which kind of screwed all of us over. It worked out better for me though because that is when the *Glee* audition came about,"[85] said McHale.

In his *Glee* audition, McHale sang the Beatles' song "Let It Be." "I auditioned pretty early on, and my callback and first audition were within two days of each other. The worst part was waiting like 6 and a half weeks until I got [called] for it. And like 'They're probably trying to find somebody else for the part, what am I going to do?' And I was hoping I didn't forget how to play the part. But luckily, it was all worth it,"[86] McHale said.

According to McHale, he and Artie share a love of singing and music, regardless of what anyone thinks. He says, however, that Artie is more confident than he was in high school, especially with girls. Although the producers thought McHale was the right actor for the role of Artie, he needed to change his appearance for the part. "We actually had to give him what we call a make-under because, you know, in this boy-band stuff, he's in his tight little T-shirts and come-hither looks, and we sort of put him in these polyester, horror-show outfits,"[87] said Murphy.

Casting an able-bodied actor instead of a disabled actor caused some controversy at first, but McHale won over many fans. He recalled,

> A mom came up to me and she said that her son was in a wheelchair, and after our pilot first aired, he would watch the show every day. And she said she felt dumb because she could not figure out why he liked the show so much. Then she realized that the show was the first time in sixteen years that her son had ever seen a character portrayed on TV in a wheelchair. So that really affected me—to know that we are actually doing something that is touching people in a real way."[88]

Tina Cohen-Chang

One of the quieter members of the glee club at William McKinley High School is Tina Cohen-Chang, played by actress Jenna Ushkowitz. Born in Seoul, Korea, Ushkowitz was adopted and raised in Long Island, New York. When she was only three years old, Ushkowitz's parents recognized that she loved being in front of the camera and performing for people. "I was kind of one of those kids who would go up to people in restaurants and say hi to all the tables—that kind of thing,"[89] Ushkowitz said. Her parents

Jenna Ushkowitz appeared in television commercials and on Broadway as a child.

got her an agent who quickly booked her for several commercials, including ones for Jell-O with comedian Bill Cosby, Fisher-Price, and Toys"R"Us.

Ushkowitz's big break came in 1996 when she got a role in the Broadway revival of the musical *The King and I*. "Five hundred kids auditioned for the role in *The King and I*. I was in the fourth grade and when I got it. I ran around school telling all my teachers,"[90] she said. Ushkowitz balanced her theater work with school, attending Holy Trinity, a performing arts high school where she played roles in several school musicals. In high school, Ushkowitz was a member of her school's show choir. This makes her the only core cast member of *Glee* who actually participated in a show choir in real life.

After high school, Ushkowitz studied acting in college, graduating from Marymount Manhattan College in 2007. After graduation, she returned to Broadway as an understudy for several roles in *Spring Awakening*, where she met future *Glee* costar Lea Michele. It would also open the door for her audition for *Glee*. "Jim Carnahan, who did some of the casting for *Glee*, brought in pretty much everyone who appeared in *Spring Awakening*. For my first audition, I didn't have to sing, and when I walked out of the room, I thought I didn't get it,"[91] said Ushkowitz. But the producers called her back to test in Los Angeles for the network, where she won the role of Tina.

Ushkowitz says she is very different from her on-screen character. "I'm not really like Tina, obviously. I don't have blue hair. Tina's really quiet and really shy, and I definitely can pull from that because I was when I was in school. But she's a little angrier than I was, and I'm a little more positive,"[92] she said.

Although Ushkowitz loves her experience with *Glee*, she hopes to someday return to the stage. "I am loving doing television, but theater is where my training is and I would love to come back,"[93] she said.

Chapter 5

The Cheerios

Not everyone at William McKinley High School is excited about the school's glee club. The Cheerios are the school's award-winning cheerleading squad. Worried that they will have to share school funding with the socially-inferior glee clubbers, the Cheerios and their coach plot to bring down the club.

The Coach

Leading the pack of *Glee*k haters is cheerleading coach, Sue Sylvester, played by actress Jane Lynch. "I came out of the womb wanting to perform and act," Lynch said. "I was not one of those people who kind of debated back and forth about what I wanted to do when I grew up. I knew what I wanted to do."[94]

Although Lynch knew she wanted to be an actress, her parents were worried that she would have a hard time finding a job. To appease them, she enrolled in Illinois State University as a mass communications major after high school. But the acting bug kept calling her. "By the end of my freshman year, I was a full-on theater major," she said. "I changed my major, and I don't think I even bothered to tell anybody."[95]

After earning her bachelor's degree, Lynch earned a master of fine arts at Cornell University in New York. Then she returned to Illinois, where she spent the next ten years performing in the prestigious Steppenwolf Theatre Company and touring with the improv comedy troupe the Second City. Second City was a training ground for other successful comedians, including Bill Murray,

Tina Fey, and Steve Carell. Lynch also toured the country as Carol Brady in *The Real Live Brady Bunch*, a stage show based on the hit television show, *The Brady Bunch* (1969–1974). These experiences helped Lynch hone her comedic skills and deadpan delivery. "Flying by the seat of your pants is what you learn doing Second City and *The Real Live Brady Bunch*. It's being open to things not going like you thought they were going to be, and to be able to flow with that and roll with that," she said. "You never knew what was going to happen, and that was part of the fun too."[96]

When she was in her thirties, Lynch moved to Los Angeles and began auditioning in Hollywood. She landed a small role in the

Jane Lynch, second from left, plays a folk singer in the 2003 comedy A Mighty Wind, one of her several movie and television roles she played before being cast in Glee.

60 The Creators and Cast of *Glee*

movie, *The Fugitive* (2003), starring Harrison Ford. Over the next several years, she steadily auditioned and worked, landing theater roles, guest spots in sitcoms, commercials, and voice-over work. At the same time, Lynch grew increasingly frustrated at the small parts. As she approached her fortieth birthday, she considered quitting acting.

Then actor and filmmaker Christopher Guest saw Lynch in a breakfast cereal commercial and recognized her comedic talent. He cast her in his next three movies: *Best in Show* (2000), *A Mighty Wind* (2003), and *For Your Consideration* (2006), in which Lynch charmed national audiences. "The man [Guest] changed my life. He blew the doors open for me,"[97] she said.

Lynch quickly became known in Hollywood as a talented character actress. She appeared in more than 130 television shows and movies, including the television shows *Married . . . with Children* (1987–1997), *The X-Files* (1993–2002), *Frasier* (1993–2004), *Friends* (1994–2004), *Gilmore Girls* (2000–2007), and *Arrested Development* (2003–2006). "There's definitely a common thread in all my characters—authoritarian, sarcastic, don't-give-people-the-benefit-of-the-doubt kind of characters. I think it's probably very good therapy, because I'm a much nicer person at home as I get it all out at work. That kind of contemptuous behavior is just below the surface for me, so it's nice I don't have to dig deep for it,"[98] said Lynch.

One of the high points in her career came when she was cast in the 2005 hit movie *The 40-Year-Old Virgin*, starring Carell as Andy. In the film, Lynch plays Andy's boss Paula, who offers to help him lose his virginity and serenades him with a silly song that Lynch improvised on the set.

When casting Sue Sylvester, the self-assured cheerleading coach with a locker full of one-liners, producers knew they wanted Lynch for the role. "There was no question, she was who Ryan and Ian and myself wanted,"[99] said *Glee* executive producer Dante De Loreto. At first, they did not plan for Sue Sylvester to be a regular character. But Brennan and Murphy quickly recognized the genius Lynch brought to the show. They wrote more for her and gave her character a backstory. Soon Sue Sylvester was terrorizing the Barbie-doll Cheerios, blackmailing the school principal, and trying her best to destroy Will Schuester and the glee club.

Lynch's deadpan delivery and comedic lines quickly made her a fan favorite, a villain who people loved. Lynch says that playing a villain like Sue Sylvester is fun. When she puts on Sue's trademark tracksuit, she suddenly has a license to say whatever she wants. "She has no filter; whatever heinous thought comes into her mind comes right out of her mouth,"[100] she said.

Lynch says that one major difference between her and the characters she plays is that she does not have the super confidence that most of them exude. In her own life, she waited until her thirties to pursue her acting dreams in Hollywood. She also did not admit to her family that she was gay until she was thirty-one. "I didn't want to be gay. . . . I wanted an easy life. And you know what? I am gay and I still have an easy life,"[101] she said.

Unlike many of her costars, Lynch was not hired because of her singing voice, and the show's writers did not include her in any of the musical numbers for several episodes. Yet Lynch wanted to tackle the challenge of a singing and dancing number. So she hummed tunes in front of the producers. Eventually, they got the hint and decided to write her into the musical numbers, one of which was a remake of Madonna's 1990 "Vogue" video.

Lynch's sharp-tongued cheerleading coach Sue Sylvester is the nemesis of Mr. Schuester and the members of New Directions.

After a career that included mostly guest roles and small parts, Lynch admits that she is enjoying the chance to settle into the regular, ongoing role of Sue, exploring the character over episodes and seasons. "I wanted to do something where I could hang my hat," Lynch said. "The nature of the work I've done lately has been three or four days here, there, and I travel a lot. I haven't had a character arc—I've basically just had scenes here and there. So when I got the opportunity to do *Glee*, I was absolutely thrilled. They've given me a life, they've given me a back story; the character gets affected by things,"[102] she said.

Lynch says that comedy is what drives her to perform and kept her going during the lean times of her career. "Making people laugh is a really fabulous thing because it means you're getting deep inside somebody, into their psyche, and their ability to look at themselves,"[103] she said.

Lynch has been recognized for her work on *Glee*, earning nominations in both 2010 and 2011 for a Golden Globe Award and an Emmy Award. She won the Emmy in 2010 and the Golden Globe in 2011.

The Former Cheerleader

When *Glee* began, Quinn Fabray was one of Sue Sylvester's cheerleaders. She initially joins the glee club to keep an eye on her boyfriend but then becomes a spy for her coach. Quinn soon finds herself enjoying the camaraderie and music in the glee club. When she becomes pregnant, the coach kicks her off the cheer squad.

Quinn Fabray is played by Dianna Agron, who was born in Savannah, Georgia. Her family moved to San Francisco when Agron was in the fifth grade. Because her father was the manager of a high-end San Francisco Hyatt hotel, the family lived in the hotel. Hotel life introduced Agron to many different people. "I got to see many walks of life—politicians, athletes, [motivational speaker] Tony Robbins. It was the ultimate fishbowl,"[104] she said.

From a young age, Agron loved to perform. She attended dance classes at age three, learning ballet, jazz, and later hip-hop danc-

Glee's Guest Stars

Glee has welcomed some very well-known and very accomplished actors and actresses as guest stars. In 2009 stage and screen actor Victor Garber, best known to television audiences for his starring role in *Alias* (2001–2006), played Will Schuester's dad and Broadway actress Debra Monk played Will's mom. Superstar singer Josh Groban also appeared as himself, poking fun at his own celebrity status and stealing the show. Other guest stars include Broadway superstar Kristin Chenoweth, actress Olivia Newton-John, actor Neil Patrick Harris, and Oscar-winning actress Gwyneth Paltrow.

For the cast members, the opportunity to work with these notable guest stars was a dream come true. According to Chris Colfer, he could barely move when he found out that Chenoweth was going to be on the show. Jenna Ushkowitz said she would like to see more Broadway stars as guests, while Lea Michele wants to work with Justin Timberlake.

Ian Brennan, Ryan Murphy, and Brad Falchuk insist they do not create characters for guest stars. Instead, they create the guest characters first and then decide who should fill the role.

Acclaimed Broadway actress Kristin Chenoweth, left, is one of several prominent stars to make guest appearances on Glee.

The Creators and Cast of *Glee*

ing. In fifth grade, Agron landed the role of Dorothy in a school production of *The Wizard of Oz*. "I grew up loving films like *Funny Face* and *Singin' in the Rain*. Finding out that I could incorporate acting, singing, and dancing [in a job] was novel to me as a kid. I did musical theater throughout school, and that paved the way,"[105] she said.

As a teen, Agron taught dance classes and saved her money. By the time she was eighteen, she had saved enough money to move to Los Angeles to pursue her dream of acting and performing. She says her family was supportive of her decision and never pressured her to try a different career, even though they knew that it would be very difficult.

Once in Los Angeles, Agron enrolled in acting classes. She auditioned for various roles, landing small parts in television shows, including *CSI: NY* (2004–), *Drake & Josh* (2004–2007), *Numb3rs* (2005–2010), *Close to Home* (2005–2007), and *Shark* (2006–2008). She also landed recurring roles on *Veronica Mars* (2004–2007) and *Heroes*.

Agron's big break came when producers cast her as Quinn Fabray in *Glee*. Ironically, Agron almost missed the audition. "I was nervous out of my mind. I was sitting in the parking lot thinking, 'Are you going to do this or are you going to walk away?'"[106] she admitted. At the time, the *Glee* casting directors were having difficulty finding the right actress to play the school's head cheerleader. The pilot was about to begin shooting, but they still had not found Quinn. When Agron finally went in for the audition, she sang "Fly Me to the Moon," a song made famous by singer Frank Sinatra. Still, the producers were not convinced she was the right actress for the role. They asked her to come back, wearing something sexier and with straight hair. Agron went to the store and bought a hair straightener, then headed to a Starbucks bathroom where she straightened her blond hair. She returned to the studio, looking just right for the part. This time, the producers realized they had found Quinn. About a week later, Agron was filming in the studio.

Although she may look the part, Agron points out one major difference between her and her Catholic character. Agron was raised Jewish. Her mother converted to Judaism before marrying

Dianna Agron won the part of popularity-conscious head cheerleader Quinn Fabray after she changed her outfit and hair at the audition to suit the producer's vision of the character.

Agron's Jewish father. Agron's parents believed it was important to share their faith with Agron and her brother when they were growing up. "I went to Sunday school, Hebrew school and a Jewish [day school] through third grade. My brother and I loved everything about Hanukkah and Passover and all the food," she said. With her busy schedule, Agron relishes family traditions and events that bring them together. "We're so scattered, so bar mitzvahs and weddings are the times we come together,"[107] she said.

Working on *Glee* has provided new opportunities for Agron. She enjoys writing and sold her first screenplay in 2008. She has also appeared in a few films, such as *Burlesque* (2010), with Christina Aguilera, Cher, and Stanley Tucci. She also starred in the 2011 action movie, *I Am Number Four*, playing teen Sarah Hart. The role is very different from the popularity-conscious Quinn Fabray, but Agron relished the chance to try something different. "I think that as an artist, the more that you can do to diversify, and kind of challenge yourself, the more you grow. Like I know that I've grown out here. I will go back to *Glee* and take what I've learned out here,"[108] Agron said while filming the movie.

Through it all, Agron tries to remember to celebrate each success along the way, no matter how small. "My goal has always been not to look forward to the next thing, but to relish and celebrate the successes I have at the moment. Whether it's landing a part in a student film or having a good day in acting class, I never discredit anything. . . . It's important to say to yourself, Today was a good day,"[109] she said.

Cheerleader Brittney

The role of cheerleader Brittney Pierce is one of *Glee*'s smaller parts. Brittney often appears with fellow cheerleader, best friend, and sometimes love interest, Santana Lopez. Brittney is played by Heather Morris, who often steals scenes with her impeccable comedic timing.

Growing up in Arizona, Morris began dancing as a toddler. She loved it and took as many classes and signed up for as many competitions as she could. After high school, Morris started classes at a local college. But dance still called to her and at age nineteen she decided to move to Los Angeles and pursue her dream of becoming a professional dancer.

After a few years, Morris made it to the semifinals of the television dance show *So You Think You Can Dance* (2005–). Unfortunately, she did not make the cut but used the rejection as motivation to keep trying. She kept auditioning, and at one project, a choreographer for music superstar Beyoncé spotted her and arranged for Morris to audition for Beyoncé's tour, *The Beyoncé Experience*. Morris got the job and became one of the dancers who performed Beyoncé's hit "Single Ladies" with her

Veteran dancer Heather Morris, who plays cheerleader Brittney Pierce, performs in one of the show's trademark elaborate production numbers.

White House Easter Egg Roll

One of the *Glee* cast's favorite memories is performing at the annual White House Easter egg–rolling contest in 2010. The actors and actresses were all excited to meet President Barack Obama and First Lady Michelle Obama. Wearing jeans and red T-shirts, they performed several group and individual numbers, including "Somebody to Love" and "Don't Stop Believin'." The catchy music was a hit, and the first family sang and danced as they watched.

when the superstar performed live several times, including on the *American Music Awards*, *Saturday Night Live* (1975–), and the *Today Show* (1952–).

For her role on *Glee*, Morris actually never auditioned. Instead, the producers brought her to the set to teach the "Single Ladies" dance to the actors. She ended up getting the part of the third cheerleader, Brittney. Morris recalled, "

I'd made the decision I was going to stop dancing—I wasn't happy, and I'd always had a dream of acting, but I was so nervous, 'cause everybody wants to be an actress. . . . I told this to the *Glee* choreographer, Zach Woodlee, and he told me he was pushing my name to Ryan Murphy, and "by chance, we're working right now on the 'Single Ladies' dance you did with Beyoncé," so I went in to teach Chris Colfer and Jenna Ushkowitz. And Ryan ended up coming in and watching me a couple times. A week later I got a call from my agent, "You're officially booked on *Glee* for Brittany."[110]

The Cheerios **69**

Cheerleader Santana

Naya Rivera, the actress who plays Santana Lopez, came to *Glee* a bit more traditionally than Morris. The Puerto Rican, German, and African American actress began acting as a child. She worked on several television shows over the years, including actor Eddie Murphy's sitcom, *The Royal Family* (1991–1992), when she was only four years old.

Naya Rivera's role as cheerleader Santana Lopez allows her to combine her love of acting and music, which she has pursued since childhood.

In addition to acting, Rivera says that she enjoys songwriting. She began writing as a teenager as an outlet for her thoughts and emotions. When *Glee* came along, Rivera immediately recognized the opportunity to combine her two interests: acting and music. Hearing that Ryan Murphy was one of the show's creators made her even more determined to win a part on the show. She auditioned and won the role of cheerleader Santana.

Ironically in real life, Rivera wanted to be a cheerleader but was too busy with her acting schedule to join the squad. "I begged my parents to let me join the cheer squad my freshman year, but in the end, I was too busy acting for the time commitment it takes to be on a squad, and I didn't want to let the other girls down," she explained. "With that said, playing a cheerleader on the show gives me a chance to fulfill my abandoned high school dreams. I absolutely *love* playing a cheerleader. I get to wear a uniform for most of my scenes, and I've had the opportunity to learn some cheer moves."[111]

Beyond getting the chance to be a cheerleader, Rivera says that her cast mates have made working on *Glee* one of the best experiences of her career. "The material itself is a joy to be a part of because we're always laughing, but the other cast members are really what make going to work every day worthwhile," she said. "Imagine being surrounded by 15 of the funniest people you know, all day, every day. That's what working on *Glee* is like. My cheeks hurt from laughing so much. That's heaven to me."[112]

Chapter 6

The Jocks

Some of the most unlikely members of the William McKinley High School glee club are jocks. Some, like Finn Hudson, join unwillingly at first, while others, like Puck Puckerman, join to impress girls. In each episode, the jocks walk a fine line between the popular crowd and the geeky glee club, learning about themselves along the way.

The Quarterback

Perhaps the hardest role to cast was that of Finn Hudson, the high school quarterback with a secret passion for singing. "It was important that Finn be a very good singer, but he also had to be a guy's guy, a strapping football star, or the character wouldn't work," said Robert Ulrich, one of the show's casting directors. "He also had to play a naïve, not stupid, quality. It was a difficult character."[113]

After much searching for Finn, newcomer Cory Monteith, with his good looks and raw talent proved to be the perfect fit. The Canadian actor was born and raised in Victoria, British Columbia, by a single mother, a similarity he shares with his character.

By age thirteen, Monteith was struggling in school. He admits to being rebellious and skipping school to drink alcohol and smoke marijuana. His mother tried sending him to different schools and alternative programs for troubled teens, but nothing worked. By the ninth grade, Monteith dropped out of school entirely.

Throughout his teens, Monteith drifted through a series of blue-collar jobs, including a Walmart greeter, a school bus driver, and a cab driver. At the same time, his drug use intensified. Afraid for his life, Monteith's mother and several friends staged an intervention when Monteith was nineteen years old. He agreed to enter a rehabilitation program but soon went back to using drugs. Monteith hit bottom, however, when he was caught stealing. "I stole a significant amount of money from a family member. I knew I was going to get caught, but I was so desperate I didn't care. It was a cry for help. I was confronted and I said, 'Yeah, it was me.' It was the first honorable, truthful thing that had come out of my mouth in years,"[114] he said.

His family gave him an ultimatum: He had to stop using drugs or they would report his crime to the police. Monteith says it was a turning point in his life. He decided it was time to take charge and make a change in his life. "I was done fighting myself. I finally said, 'I'm gonna start looking at my life and figure out why I'm doing this,"[115] he said.

Monteith Starts Acting

Monteith quit using drugs; moved in with a family friend in Nanaimo, Canada; and got a job as a roofer. Then a friend suggested that he try acting. So Monteith enrolled in his first acting class and fell in love with it. With the encouragement of his acting coach, Monteith moved to Vancouver, a popular filming location for big-budget Hollywood films and television shows, to pursue a career. He also took a job as a waiter to earn money while he pursued acting. He auditioned for many parts, landing small roles in movies, such as *Final Destination 3* (2006) and *Deck the Halls* (2006), and in television shows, including *Smallville* (2001–2011) and *Kyle XY* (2006–2009).

When Monteith's manager told him about *Glee*, he was uncertain about his chances of being cast. In his twenties, he was a lot older than a high school student. In addition, the show wanted

Cory Monteith plays quarterback Finn Hudson, a jock with a passion for singing.

people with singing and dancing experience. Monteith had neither. He liked music and had even played drums in a band when he was seventeen years old, but he had no professional experience or training. After deciding he had nothing to lose, Monteith made an audition tape and sent it in to the *Glee* casting directors. Instead of singing on the tape, Monteith drummed with pencils on the back of Tupperware boxes. "I looked like a dork, making all these faces, banging on Tupperware like an idiot,"[116] he said.

Although Monteith's audition tape was unconventional, the casting directors saw his potential. They asked for a second tape, this time with him singing. Monteith complied, and the second tape displayed his raw talent. The producers had seen many actors audition for the role of Finn, and many of them were polished professionals. None of them fit their image of the wholesome football player who becomes a glee club singer. The producers asked Monteith to come to Los Angeles so that they could meet him in person. Monteith sang Billy Joel's classic rock song, "Honesty." It was a smart choice because it fit Finn's personality, and he won the role.

Monteith Learns to Sing

Before *Glee*, Monteith never considered himself a singer. He sang with the radio in the car, or in the shower, but not professionally. Now that he was Finn, Monteith needed to learn the show's musical numbers each week, which meant not only learning the songs, but also the choreography for the dancing. For the first time, he would also be spending time in a recording studio, recording songs for each episode. At first, he had a lot to learn. "Cory had never sung in the [recording] studio in his life before [he sang] 'Don't Stop Believin'. The first time we recorded, he didn't know how to breathe and sing at the same time; he almost passed out. To see where he is now is like night and day; he's come so far,"[117] said Adam Anders, *Glee*'s music producer. With vocal coaching and a lot of rehearsal, Monteith's musical talent blossomed. "Cory's growth as a singer was tremendous. He's become an amazing singer,"[118] said Ulrich.

The Jocks **75**

Monteith, performing during the live Glee touring show in 2011, had no professional experience or training as a singer before landing the role of Finn.

76 The Creators and Cast of *Glee*

Harry Shum Jr.

Actor Harry Shum Jr. plays Mike Chang, a football player who cannot sing. Born in Costa Rica, Shum moved to California with his parents and two sisters at age five. He discovered the stage in high school, when a friend dared him to join the school's dance team. Soon, he was hooked, attending dance classes and watching music videos.

In 2002 Shum was cast as the only male dancer on an episode of the comedy show *ComicView* (1992–2008). He has performed as a dancer on tour with Beyoncé, Jennifer Lopez, Mariah Carey, and Jessica Simpson. He danced as a silhouette in iPod commercials. He also worked as a dancer and choreographer for the Legion of Extraordinary Dancers, a group that performed on the television show *So You Think You Can Dance* (2005–) in 2009 and at the 82nd Academy Awards in 2010.

When Shum heard about Ryan Murphy's idea for a singing and dancing television show, he thought it might be a cool project. He admits, however, that he had no idea that it would become so popular or last more than a few episodes. Since his debut, Shum's character, Mike, has taken a larger role in the show, becoming a key member of New Directions.

Harry Shum Jr., a veteran dancer and choreographer, plays football player Mike Chang.

The Jocks

When talking about his character, Monteith says that he understands Finn, even though the two of them are different. His least favorite thing about Finn is that he is often the last person to realize things. "Finn is almost as smart as rocks. I like playing that. To prepare Finn before a scene, I just stop thinking! (kidding . . . kind of.),"[119] Monteith joked.

With *Glee*'s success, Monteith admits that his life has become a bit of a whirlwind. Yet he feels lucky and tries to keep everything in perspective. "The fact that I get to do this [acting] for a living is ridiculous. I still can't wrap my head around the fact that people are paying me to do this. . . . Things went very, very badly in my life for a long time and now they are going very well,"[120] he said.

The Bad Boy Football Jock

Fans first glimpsed football jock Noah "Puck" Puckerman, played by actor Mark Salling, when he dumped Kurt Hummel into a school dumpster. His reputation as a bad boy did not improve when viewers discovered that he was the father of Quinn Fabray's baby. Quinn just happened to be the girlfriend of his best buddy Finn Hudson. Yet as the show developed, so did Puck's character, sometimes showing a softer side. For Salling, balancing Puck's two sides is the challenge. "There needs to be a combination of both. He wouldn't be Puck if he wasn't a badass, but he wouldn't be accessible if he didn't grow as a character. I just hope the character's funny. I want him to be comic relief,"[121] said Salling.

Growing up in Texas, Salling was interested in music for as long as he can remember. He started playing the piano at age five and later learned to play the guitar, bass, and drums. By age seven, he was writing his own songs. He also tried acting, landing small roles in a Heineken commercial, the television show *Walker, Texas Ranger* (1993–2001), and the movie *Children of the Corn IV* (1996).

Mark Salling cut his hair in a Mohawk to audition for the role of Noah "Puck" Puckerman, a look that helped him land the part.

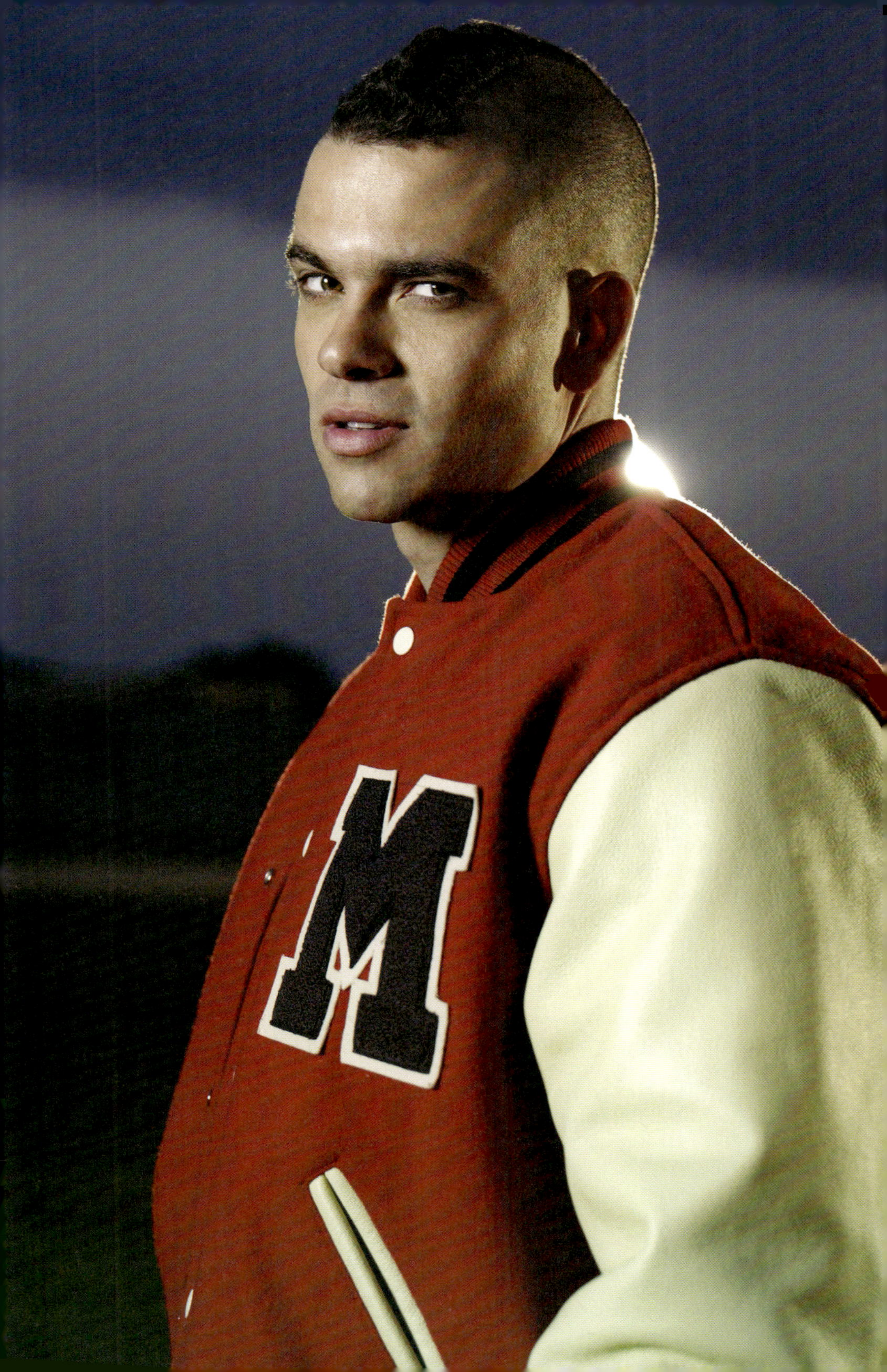

After Salling graduated from high school, he moved to Los Angeles and enrolled in the LA Music Academy. "I came up to California to attend a music school and started playing as a guitar player in bands as a session player. I was kind of struggling to make ends meet by just teaching lessons and playing as a guitar player,"[122] he said.

After seven years without a big break, Salling considered moving home to Austin, Texas, and trying the music scene there. Before he left California, however, he decided to give acting another try. He enrolled in an acting class and hired an agent. "I finally decided to get an agent to try to land some roles as an actor to pay the bills. I was out of money and was about to pack it up and go back to Texas when my agent called and told me I

The *Glee* Project

Glee's popularity has given rise to its own reality competition show, *The Glee Project*. The show premiered on the Oxygen network in June 2011. After an initial audition process, twelve contestants compete over a series of weeks to earn a guest role on *Glee*. Each weekly episode centers on a theme, such as individuality or theatricality. Contestants are given a homework assignment to learn and practice a chosen song. They also have to prepare a music video, learning choreography and recording audio tracks in a recording studio. The contestants' performances are overseen by *Glee's* casting director Robert Ulrich. Each week, the bottom-performing contestant is eliminated from the competition.

Throughout its first season, the show's audience grew. By the final episode, which aired on August 21, 2011, approximately 1.2 million viewers tuned in to see the first season's results. Contestants Damian McGinty and Samuel Larson both won a seven-episode guest spot on *Glee*. Runners-up Lindsay Pearce and Alex Newell will also be starring in a two-episode arc on *Glee*. Based on the reality show's success, Oxygen is already setting up casting calls for a second season of *The Glee Project*.

was going to read for *Glee*. It was pretty surreal and all happened pretty fast,"[123] Salling said.

When he read the script, Salling knew that he wanted to role of Puck. He wanted it so badly in fact, that he lied at the audition and told the producers that he was nineteen years old, when he was actually twenty-seven. He also used his hair to stand out, arriving at the *Glee* auditions with a Mohawk. Salling had it cut that way a few months earlier and decided it might help him stand out from the other actors. He was right, and he got the role. He did not know then that the Mohawk would become part of Puck's recognizable character. "I'm so over the Mohawk, I'm not gonna lie. . . . It was cool for a while, but I've had it for like a year, you know I'm kind of over it,"[124] Salling admitted.

Shooting an episode of *Glee* is a lot of work. Because the show's writers are only about one to two scripts ahead of filming, the cast usually does not get a script until about a week before they need to start shooting the episode. The cast has to quickly learn everything, including lines, choreography, and music. "It's quite a workload to be honest. Some days we might have to get up early for dance rehearsals and then go shoot some scenes and then later head to the studio to do pre records for the singing scenes. It's pretty grueling,"[125] Salling said. At the same time, he is learning a lot from the talent around him. "It's opened my horizons to so many different types of music and an appreciation for dancers and the people behind the scenes—the producers and the writers and everything. . . . So the show all around has been a really enlightening artistic experience, just for me as a person and artist. I try to take as much of it in and learn as much as I can, and I have,"[126] Salling said.

Salling's Interests

When he is not working on *Glee*, Salling likes to play basketball, Frisbee golf, and Ping-Pong. He also sketches, especially nature and birds. He says that he has always been interested in ornithology, the study of birds, and he volunteers at a local bird rehabilitation center in California. Salling says that if he was not working as an actor or a musician, he probably would have been working with animals, either as a veterinarian or running his own rehabilitation clinic.

Yet Salling's main passion remains music. Before he joined the cast of *Glee*, Salling released his debut album, *Smoke Signals*, under the stage name Jericho in February 2008. He produced and recorded the album by himself, as well as doing all the instrumentation and vocals.

In October 2010 Salling released a solo album titled *Pipe Dreams*. "Pipe dreams is a term that represents what people will tell you are unrealistic dreams. That's kind of what me considering a career in music and moving out west was—a pipe dream,"[127] said Salling about his album's title. He included a variety of sounds on the album to give listeners a better sense of who he is as an artist. He explained,

> I kind of wanted to show a little bit of diversity in the sound. Overall it's got pop melodies over jazz chord changes with a rock feel, I'd say. . . . Some are darker than others. Some are optimistic and some are pessimistic. I think it all documents where I was in my life at the time or the mood I was in. Sometimes my outlook on things is very positive and sometimes it's not. I think overall the record will really give people an insight to who I am."[128]

Salling is also using his newfound *Glee* fame to give back to the community. In late 2011 he announced his partnership with ConAgra Foods and its Child Hunger Ends Here campaign to raise awareness about child hunger in the United States. According to the campaign, nearly one in four children in the United States does not have enough food to live an active, healthy life. "Child hunger is something we think of as a foreign issue and it's a huge issue right here in the United States. 17 million kids are affected. Actually, my native state of Texas is number two on that list, so I feel a personal connection,"[129] said Salling. He is thankful that *Glee*'s success has given him the opportunity to help. "That's one of the benefits of this wonderful show that I've been fortunate to be part of. It gives you a platform and a voice for causes that you feel passionate about."[130]

The Future of *Glee*

The future looks bright for *Glee*. Only time will tell how long the show will have its hold on *Glee*ks around the world or if the actors who found fame on *Glee* can successfully make the leap to other projects.

Meanwhile Murphy and the other producers plan to keep incorporating new characters and finding fresh new faces for *Glee*. "I think the fun thing about the show is it's a celebration of youth and talent and I think that just like with the original cast, I think finding those young unknown people and giving them an opportunity to break into the business and become stars is a really fun and exciting thing and is the spirit of the series,"[131] said Murphy.

Notes

Introduction: A Successful Musical Comedy

1. Quoted in Aly Semigran. "'*Glee*' Wins Big at Golden Globes." MTV, January 16, 2011. www.mtv.com/news/articles/1656082/glee-3-wins-golden-globes.jhtml.
2. Quoted in Shirley Halperin. "Exclusive: Inside the Hot Business of '*Glee*.'" *Hollywood Reporter*, January 25, 2011. www.hollywoodreporter.com/news/hot-business-glee-75593.
3. Quoted in Craig McLean. "*Glee*: The Making of a Musical Phenomenon." *Telegraph*, January 24, 2011. www.telegraph.co.uk/culture/8271318/*Glee*-the-making-of-a-musical-phenomenon.html.

Chapter 1: Building a Breakout Show

4. Quoted in Colleen Mastony. "'*Glee* Club' TV Series Creator Uses Mt. Prospect High School for Inspiration." *Chicago Tribune*, September 8, 2009. http://articles.chicagotribune.com/2009-09-08/entertainment/0909070170_1_show-choir-glee-ryan-murphy.
5. Quoted in Mastony. "'*Glee* Club' TV Series Creator Uses Mt. Prospect High School for Inspiration."
6. Quoted in Todd VanDerWerff. "Interview: Ian Brennan, Co-Creator of *Glee*." A.V. Club, February 4, 2011. www.avclub.com/articles/ian-brennan-cocreator-of-glee,51326/.
7. Quoted in Mastony. "'*Glee* Club' TV Series Creator Uses Mt. Prospect High School for Inspiration."
8. Quoted in "The Musical Magic of '*Glee*.'" NPR, September 11, 2009. www.npr.org/templates/transcript/transcript.php?storyId=112721367.
9. Quoted in "The Musical Magic of *Glee*."
10. Quoted in Tim Stack. "*Glee*." *Entertainment Weekly*, September 18, 2009.
11. Quoted in Mickey O'Connor. "Ryan Murphy on *Glee*: People Don't Just Break out into Song; 'There Are Rules.'" *TV Guide*, May 19, 2009. www.tvguide.com/News/Ryan-Murphy-Glee-1006181.aspx.

12. Quoted in Michael Schneider. "Fox Greenlights '*Glee*' Pilot." *Variety*, July 23, 2008. www.variety.com/article/VR1117989408?refCatId=14.
13. Quoted in Lisa Respers France. "'*Glee*' Banks on Risky Strategy." CNN.com, September 22, 2009. www.cnn.com/2009/SHOWBIZ/TV/09/16/glee.tv.show/index.html.
14. Mary McNamara. "'*Glee*' on Fox." *Los Angeles Times*, May 19, 2009. http://articles.latimes.com/print/2009/may/19/entertainment/et-glee19.
15. Quoted in Stack. "*Glee*."
16. Quoted in France. "*Glee* Banks on Risky Strategy."
17. Quoted in Tim Stack. "*Glee* the Show Heard 'Round the World." *Entertainment Weekly*, May 28, 2010.
18. Quoted in "'*Glee*' Returns as a Cult and Musical Success." CBSNews.com, April 12, 2010. www.cbsnews.com/stories/2010/04/12/entertainment/main6389066.shtml.
19. Quoted in "*Glee* Returns as a Cult and Musical Success."
20. Quoted in Stack, "*Glee* the Show Heard 'Round the World."
21. Quoted in Curtis Silver, "We're All *Glee*ks—10 Questions for *Glee* Co-Creator Brad Falchuk." *Wired*, December 7, 2009. www.wired.com/geekdad/2009/12/were-all-gleeks-10-questions-with-glee-co-creator-brad-falchuk/.

Chapter 2: The Lynchpin

22. Quoted in "Casting the Keys to *Glee*." Emmys, November 1, 2009. www.emmys.com/articles/casting-keys-glee.
23. Quoted in Claire Hoffman. "Hot for Teacher: Matthew Morrison." *Details*, December 2010. www.details.com/celebrities-entertainment/cover-stars/201012/fox-glee-actor-Will-Schuester-teacher-singer-matthew-morrison#ixzz1Z45vZTOa.
24. Quoted in Hoffman, "Hot for Teacher."
25. 2Quoted in "Matthew Morrison: 'I Want To Do It All.'" *Parade*, November 29, 2009. www.parade.com/celebrity/2009/11/matthew-morrison.html.
26. Quoted in "Matthew Morrison: 'I Want To Do It All.'"
27. Quoted in Michael Lavine. "Will Schuester: The Hot Teacher." *Glee* Special Issue, *People*, October 2010 pp. 28–29.
28. Quoted in "Matthew Morrison: 'I Want To Do It All.'"

29. Quoted in Kelley L. Carter. "Broadway Star Morrison Gets All Keyed Up for '*Glee*.'" *USA Today*, May 18, 2009. www.usatoday.com/life/people/2009-05-17-matthew-morrison_N.htm.
30. Quoted in Hoffman. "Hot for Teacher."
31. Quoted in "Matthew Morrison: 'I Want To Do It All.'"
32. Quoted in Elysa Gardner. "Morrison Lets People in on Who I Am with His First Solo Album." *USA Today*, May 9, 2011.
33. Quoted in Gardner. "Morrison Lets People in on Who I Am with His First Solo Album."
34. Quoted in Gardner. "Morrison Lets People in on Who I Am with His First Solo Album."
35. Quoted in "Matthew Morrison: 'I Want To Do It All.'"
36. Quoted in "Matthew Morrison Reflects on '*Glee*'s' Success Before His Concert Tour Kicks Off." *Los Angeles Times*, April 21, 2011. http://latimesblogs.latimes.com/showtracker/2011/04/matthew-morrison-reflects-on-glees-success-before-his-concert-tour-takes-off.html.
37. Quoted in "Matthew Morrison Reflects on '*Glee*'s' Success Before His Concert Tour Kicks Off."
38. Quoted in "Matthew Morrison: 'I Want To Do It All.'"
39. Quoted in "Interview: Jessalyn Gilsig (Terri Schuester) from *Glee*." The TV Chick, October 28, 2009. http://thetvchick.com/glee/interview-jessalyn-gilsig-terri-schuester-from-glee/.
40. Quoted in Joan Wagner. "The Woman *Glee* Fans Love to Hate." Oprah, November 11, 2009. http://www.oprah.com/entertainment/*Glee*s-Jessalyn-Gilsig#ixzz1Z4J7U9xi.
41. Quoted in Wagner. "The Woman *Glee* Fans Love to Hate."
42. Quoted in "Interview: Jessalyn Gilsig (Terri Schuester) from *Glee*."
43. Quoted in Amy Friedman. "From Grundy to '*Glee*.'" *Roanoke Times*, April 7, 2010. www.roanoke.com/theedge/stories/wb/242430.
44. Quoted in Friedman. "From Grundy to '*Glee*.'"
45. Quoted in Jamie Steinberg. "Jayma Mays: *Glee*ful." Starry Constellation Magazine, http://starrymag.com/content.asp?ID=4318&CATEGORY=INTERVIEWS.
46. Quoted in Steinberg. "Jayma Mays: *Glee*ful."
47. Quoted in "Exclusive Interview: Jayma Mays (Emma) from *Glee*." The TV Chick, December 2, 2009. http://thetvchick

.com/exclusive-interviews/exclusive-interview-jayma-mays-emma-from-glee/.
48. Quoted in Friedman. "From Grundy to '*Glee*.'"

Chapter 3: The Driving Force

49. Quoted in Donna Freydkin. "Lea Michele Never Stopped Believing." *USA Today,* May 10, 2010. www.usatoday.com/life/people/2010-05-10-LeaMichele10_CV_N.htm.
50. Quoted in Richard Huff. "'*Glee*' Star Lea Michele Thrilled by Leap from Broadway to New Fox Show." NYDailyNews.com, August 30, 2009. www.nydailynews.com/entertainment/tv/2009/08/30/2009-08-30_glee_is_the_word_njraised_actress_thrilled_by_leap_from_bway_to_hot_tv_role.html.
51. Quoted in Josh Patner. "Lea Michele Little Miss Big-Time." *Glamour.* www.glamour.com/sex-love-life/2010/09/lea-michele-little-miss-big-time.
52. Quoted in Robert Diamond. "Spring (Awakening) Fever: An Interview with Lea Michele." Broadwayworld.com, January 23, 2007. http://broadwayworld.com/article/Spring_Awakening_Fever_An_Interview_with_Lea_Michele_20070123.
53. Quoted in Jessica Henderson. "Get Your *Glee*k On!" *Marie claire,* April 12, 2011. www.marieclaire.com/celebrity-lifestyle/celebrities/glee-stars-interview-4.
54. Quoted in Diamond. "Spring (Awakening) Fever."
55. Quoted in Michael D. Ayers. "Interview: *Glee* Star Lea Michele on Central Park, Comedy, and a Sweaty Co-Star." The Village Voice, September 9, 2009. http://blogs.villagevoice.com/music/2009/09/interview_glee.php.
56. Quoted in Ayers. "Interview: *Glee* Star Lea Michele on Central Park, Comedy, and a Sweaty Co-Star."
57. Quoted in Henderson. "Get Your *Glee*k On!"
58. Quoted in Freydkin. "Lea Michele Never Stopped Believing."
59. Quoted in Michael Buckley. "Stage to Screens: '*Glee*' on TV; Michele & Morrison." Playbill.com, September 8, 2009. http://www.playbill.com/features/article/132637-STAGE-TO-SCREENS-*Glee*-on-TV-Michele--Morrison/all.
60. Quoted in Freydkin. "Lea Michele Never Stopped Believing."
61. Quoted in Huff. "'*Glee*' Star Lea Michele Thrilled by Leap from Broadway to New Fox Show."

62. Quoted in Freydkin. "Lea Michele Never Stopped Believing."
63. Quoted in Cristina Kinon. "Hot New Yorker: Lea Michele's Success has Bronx Feeling 'Glee.'" NYDailyNews.com, December 27, 2009. http://articles.nydailynews.com/2009-12-27/entertainment/17940697_1_lea-michele-glee-hollywood-hot-list.
64. Quoted in Kathleen Perricone. "Lea Michele on Leaving 'Glee': 'It's All Good! It's Going to Make Season 3 Amazing!'." NYDailyNews.com, July 14, 2011. www.nydailynews.com/entertainment/tv/2011/07/14/2011-07-14_lea_michele_on_leaving_glee_its_all_good_its_going_to_make_season_3_amazing.html.
65. Quoted in Marshall Heyman. "Lea Michele in Bloom." Harper's Bazaar, August 3, 2011. www.harpersbazaar.com/magazine/cover/lea-michele-interview.

Chapter 4: The *Glee* Club

66. Quoted in "Casting the Keys to Glee."
67. Quoted in "Biography." AmberRiley.net http://amberriley.net/wp/amber-riley-the-information/bio/.
68. Quoted in Dan French. "Q&A: Glee's Amber Riley." Digital spy. January 5, 2010. www.digitalspy.com/british-tv/s57/glee/tubetalk/a193784/qa-glees-amber-riley.html.
69. Quoted in French. "Q&A: *Glee*'s Amber Riley."
70. Quoted in Lisa Ingrassia. "*Glee*'s Amber Riley: 'I Love My Body.'" *People*, May 17, 2010. www.people.com/people/archive/article/0,,20367254,00.html.
71. Quoted in Ingrassia, "*Glee*'s Amber Riley."
72. Quoted in Ingrassia. "*Glee*'s Amber Riley."
73. Quoted in French. "Q&A: *Glee*'s Amber Riley."
74. Quoted in Henderson. "Get Your *Glee*k On!"
75. Quoted in Maria Elena Fernandez. "Chris Colfer's Journey from Small Town to '*Glee*.'" *Los Angeles Times*, September 8, 2009. http://latimesblogs.latimes.com/showtracker/2009/09/glee-creator-and-executive-producer-ryan-murphy-discovered-chris-colfer-but-dont-tell-the-young-actor-that-it-makes-him-feel.html.
76. Quoted in Fernandez. "Chris Colfer's Journey from Small Town to '*Glee*.'"
77. Quoted in Fernandez. "Chris Colfer's Journey from Small

Notes **89**

77. ...Town to 'Glee.'"
78. Quoted in "Casting the Keys to *Glee*."
79. Quoted in Lesley Goldberg. "Just One of the Guys." *Advocate*, October 6, 2009. www.advocate.com/Arts_and_Entertainment/Television/*Glee*s_Chris_Colfer__Just_one_of_the_guys/.
80. Quoted in Fernandez. "Chris Colfer's Journey from Small Town to '*Glee*.'"
81. Quoted in Goldberg. "Just One of the Guys."
82. Quoted in Rae Votta. "Chris Colfer on Emmys, Season 3 '*Glee*' Hopes and Hip Rotations." The Huffington Post, August 22, 2011. www.huffingtonpost.com/2011/08/21/chris-colfer-interview_n_932501.html.
83. Quoted in "Exclusive Interview: Kevin McHale (Artie) from *Glee*." The TV Chick, May 18, 2010. http://thetvchick.com/exclusive-interviews/exclusive-interview-kevin-mchale-artie-from-glee/.
84. Quoted in Catriona Wightman. "'*Glee*' Lea Michele, Chris Colfer Interview: 'Barbra Streisand Should not Be a Guest Star'." Digital spy, September 19, 2011. www.digitalspy.com/tv/s57/glee/interviews/a336704/glee-lea-michele-chris-colfer-interview-barbra-streisand-should-not-be-a-guest-star.html.
85. Quoted in Julie Miller. "Kevin McHale on *Glee*'s Wheelchair Controversy, His Dream TV Role and Celebrity *Glee*ks." Movieline, May 18, 2010. www.movieline.com/2010/05/kevin-mchale-on-glees-wheelchair-controversy-his-dream-tv-role-and-celebrity-gleeks.php?page=all.
86. Quoted in "Exclusive Interview: Kevin McHale (Artie) from *Glee*."
87. Quoted in "The Musical Magic of '*Glee*.'"
88. Quoted in Miller. "Kevin McHale on *Glee*'s Wheelchair Controversy, His Dream TV Role and Celebrity *Glee*ks."
89. Quoted in "Jenna Ushkowitz Interview—JustJared.com Exclusive." JustJared.com, November 18, 2009. http://justjared.buzznet.com/2009/11/18/jenna-ushkowitz-interview/.
90. Quoted in "*Glee*'s Jenna Ushkowitz Gets Cozy for Winter." *OK!*, January 20, 2011. www.okmagazine.com/2011/01/in-this-issue-glees-jenna-ushkowitz-gets-cozy-for-winter/.

91. Quoted in Brian Scott Lipton. "Jenna Ushkowitz Is Filled with *Glee*." Theater Mania.com, November 3, 2009. www.theatermania.com/new-york/news/11-2009/jenna-ushkowitz-is-filled-with-glee_22499.html.
92. Quoted in Gabrielle Cord-Cruz, Maggie Cotter, and Ganesh Ravichandran. "Kidsday Talks with '*Glee*'s' Jenna Ushkowitz." ExploreLI, January 9, 2010. http://long-island.newsday.com/kids/kidsday-talks-with-glee-s-jenna-ushkowitz-1.1693395.
93. Quoted in Lipton. "Jenna Ushkowitz Is Filled with *Glee*."

Chapter 5: The Cheerios

94. Quoted in Kari Forsee. "The Genius of Jane Lynch." Oprah, December 21, 2009. www.oprah.com/entertainment/The-Genius-of-Jane-Lynch#ixzz1Z4K2z2mE.
95. Quoted in Forsee. "The Genius of Jane Lynch."
96. Quoted in Forsee. "The Genius of Jane Lynch,"
97. Quoted in Danielle Berrin. "Jane Lynch: I'm Just a Goof." *Guardian*, January 8, 2010. www.guardian.co.uk/tv-and-radio/2010/jan/09/jane-lynch-glee-interview.
98. Quoted in Tracey Perkins. "Jane Lynch: 'I Didn't Want to Be Gay—I Wanted an Easy Life." Mirror.co.uk, January 31, 2010. www.mirror.co.uk/celebs/celebs-on-sunday/2010/01/31/jane-lynch-i-didn-t-want-to-be-gay-i-wanted-an-easy-life-115875-21997135/.
99. Quoted in Gina Piccalo, "*Glee*'s Jane Lynch: Interview," *Telegraph*, January 10, 2011. www.telegraph.co.uk/culture/tvandradio/8223859/*Glee*s-Jane-Lynch-interview.html.
100. Quoted in Berrin. "Jane Lynch: I'm Just a Goof."
101. Quoted in Perkins. "Jane Lynch: 'I Didn't Want to Be Gay—I Wanted an Easy Life."
102. Quoted in "Meet '*Glee*' Star Jane Lynch, TV's New Queen of Mean." NPR, October 7, 2009. http://www.npr.org/templates/story/story.php?storyId=113513827.
103. Quoted in Berrin. "Jane Lynch: I'm Just a Goof."
104. Quoted in Lauren Waterman, "Dianna Agron," *Interview*. www.interviewmagazine.com/film/dianna-agron/.
105. Quoted in Suzanne Zuckerman. "Dreaming Big: Dianna Agron of *Glee*." *Women's Health*, January 28, 2010. www.womenshealthmag.com/life/dianna-agron.

106. Quoted in Zuckerman. "Dreaming Big."
107. Quoted in Gerri Miller. "*Glee* Club Glory." *JVibe*, August 2009. www.jvibe.com/Pop_culture/*Glee*.php.
108. Quoted in Steve Weintraub. "Dianna Agron on Set Interview I Am Number Four." Collider.com, October 11, 2010. http://collider.com/dianna-agron-interview-i-am-number-four/53766/.
109. Quoted in Zuckerman. "Dreaming Big."
110. Quoted in Rebecca Milzoff. "Heather Morris on Playing *Glee*'s Resident Dummy, Brittney." NYMag.com, April 13, 2010. http://nymag.com/daily/entertainment/2010/04/heather_morris_on_playing_glee.html.
111. Quoted in "Time out With: Naya Rivera from '*Glee*.'" American Cheerleader. www.americancheerleader.com/2009/09/time-out-with-naya-rivera-from-glee/.
112. Quoted in "Time out With: Naya Rivera from '*Glee*.'"

Chapter 6: The Jocks

113. Quoted in "Casting the Keys to *Glee*."
114. Quoted in Shawna Malcom. "Cory Monteith's Turning Point." *Parade*, June 24, 2011. www.parade.com/celebrity/2011/06/cory-monteith-glee.html.
115. Quoted in Malcom. "Cory Monteith's Turning Point."
116. Quoted in Erik Hedegaard. "*Glee* Gone Wild." *Rolling Stone*, May 15, 2010. pp. 42–49.
117. Quoted in Sarah Jones. "Music: The Joy of '*Glee*." Mix, January 1, 2010. http://mixonline.com/recording/mixing/music-joy-glee-0110//index.html.
118. Quoted in "Casting the Keys to *Glee*."
119. Quoted in Melody Simpson. "Meet Cory Monteith & Naya Rivera of *Glee*." Hollywood the Write Way, March 17, 2009. www.hollywoodthewriteway.com/2009/03/meet-cory-monteith-naya-rivera-of-glee.html.
120. Quoted in Marc Malkin. "*Glee*'s Cory Monteith: High School Dropout to Hollywood Star." E! Online, September 9, 2009. http://www.eonline.com/news/marc_malkin/glees_cory_monteith_high_school_dropout/143175.
121. Quoted in Neha Gandhi. "Exclusive Interview: *Glee*'s Mark Salling" *Seventeen*. www.seventeen.com/entertainment/features/mark-salling-interview.

122. Quoted in Angela Lee. "Mark Salling Interview." *Portrait*, October 2009. www.portraitmagazine.net/interviews/marksalling.html.
123. Quoted in "CT Celebrity Interview with *Glee*'s Mark Salling." Campus Talk Magazine. November 17, 2009. http://mycampustalk.com/ct-celebrity-interview-with-glees-mark-salling/.
124. Quoted in Aileen Wong. "*Glee*'s Mark Salling on His Hair: "I Hate the Mohawk." *People*, December 7, 2009. http://stylenews.peoplestylewatch.com/2009/12/07/glees-mark-salling-on-his-hair-i-hate-the-mohawk/.
125. Quoted in "CT Celebrity Interview with *Glee*'s Mark Salling."
126. Quoted in Catriona Wightman. "'*Glee*' Mark Salling, Ashley Fink Interview: 'Puck Will Never Settle Down'." Digital spy, September 16, 2011. www.digitalspy.com/tv/s57/glee/interviews/a339179/glee-mark-salling-ashley-fink-interview-puck-will-never-settle-down.html.
127. Quoted in Robbie Daw. "Mark Salling: The Idolator Interview." Idolator, October 22, 2010. http://idolator.com/5663271/mark-salling-idolator-interview.
128. Quoted in Daw. "Mark Salling."
129. Quoted in Erin Hill. "*Glee*'s Mark Salling: 'I'm Reliving High School.'" *Parade*, September 1, 2011. www.parade.com/celebrity/celebrity-parade/2011/09/mark-salling-glee.html.
130. Quoted in Hill. "*Glee*'s Mark Salling."
131. Quoted in Tim Stack. "'*Glee*' Scoop: Ryan Murphy Says He's Planning for the Show's Characters to Graduate This Season." *Entertainment Weekly*, June 20, 2011. http://insidetv.ew.com/2011/06/20/glee-ryan-murphy-graduation/.

Important Dates

1999

Ryan Murphy enters the television world as the creator and producer of the teen comedy, *Popular*.

2004

Ryan Murphy wins an Emmy Award for directing the television series *Nip/Tuck*.

2005

Ian Brennan writes a movie screenplay about a high school choir.

2008

Ian Brennan, Ryan Murphy, and Brad Falchuk rewrite Brennan's screenplay into a television pilot and pitch the show to the Fox network, which accepts it the same day.

2009

The pilot episode of *Glee* airs on May 19. The show wins five Satellite Awards.

2010

Glee wins the Golden Globe Award for Best Television Series, Comedy or Musical and four Emmy Awards. The cast of *Glee* embarks on a sold-out summer concert tour. In September, the show's second season premieres.

2011

Glee wins the Golden Globe Award for Best Television Series, Comedy or Musical and two Emmy Awards. *Glee* sells out a second North American tour and adds a summer European tour. In August, FOX releases a concert film, *Glee: The 3D Concert Movie*. In September, the show's third season premieres.

2012

Glee receives its third Golden Globe Award nomination for Best Television Series, Comedy or Musical.

For More Information

Books

Erin Balser and Suzanne Gardner. *Don't Stop Believin', The Unofficial Guide to Glee.* Toronto, CA: ECW Press, 2010. This book includes biographies of the *Glee* cast and synopses of the episodes from the show's first season.

Sarah Oliver. *The Completely Unofficial Glee A to Z.* New York: John Blake, 2010. This book is packed with photos and trivia about *Glee* and its cast.

Amy Rickman. *Gleeful! A Totally Unofficial Guide to the Hit TV Series Glee.* New York: Villard Books, 2010. This book is a behind-the-scenes look at the creators, cast, and music of *Glee*, including detailed biographies and little-known trivia about the cast and creators.

Leah Wilson. *Filled with Glee: The Unauthorized Glee Companion.* Dallas, TX: Smart Pop, 2010. This book includes instructions on how to put together a glee club, a season-one episode guide, detailed song lists, and trivia.

Internet Sources

Paula Hendrickson. "Casting the Keys to *Glee*." *Emmys*. November 1, 2009. www.emmys.com/articles/casting-keys-*Glee*.

"The Musical Magic of '*Glee*.'" *NPR*, September 11, 2009. www.npr.org/templates/transcript/transcript.php?storyId=112721367.

"TV's Most Talked About Show: The Cast of *Glee*." *Oprah*. April 7, 2010. www.oprah.com/showinfo/TVs-Most-Talked-About-Show-The-Cast-of-*Glee*.

Websites

Entertainment Weekly (www.ew.com). This is the website for *Entertainment Weekly* magazine. It offers information on everyone and everything in the world of entertainment, including the latest news about *Glee* and its cast.

***Glee* on FOX** (www.fox.com/glee). This is the website for the FOX television network. It offers official information about *Glee*. Visitors can view full episodes and video clips.

People (www.people.com). This is the website of *People* magazine. It offers news and features about the cast of *Glee* and other celebrities.

Index

A
Agron, Dianna, 63, 65, *66*, 67
American Idol, 16, 17, 48
Awards and nominations, 6–7, 8
  Colfer and, 53
  Groff and, 38
  Lynch and, 63
  Michele and, 39, 44–45
  Morrison and, 25
  for *Nip/Tuck,* 13

B
Beyoncé, 68, 69
Billboard Hot 100, 8
Brennan, Ian, 9–11, *10, 14*
  Sylvester and, 61
  writing process, 14

C
Cast, *7, 16–17,* 22, *43*
  difficulties finding, 23, 47
  marketing show, 18–19, *19,* 20
  shooting episodes, 81
  on tour, 22, *22, 51*
  White House Easter egg roll, 69
  See also individual members
Characters
  Abrams, Artie, 55, *55*
  Anderson, Blaine, 54
  Berry, Rachel, 35, *36, 41,* 42, 45
  Chang, Mike, 77, *77*
  Cohen-Chang, Tina, 57, *57*
  Fabray, Quinn, 63, 78
  Hudson, Finn, 72, *74,* 78
  Hummel, Burt, 50, *50*
  Hummel, Kurt, 49, 52, 54
  Jones, Mercedes, 46
  Lopez, Santana, 70, *70*
  Pierce, Brittany, 67, *68*
  Pillsbury, Emma, 33, *33,* 34
  Puckerman, Noah "Puck", 78, *79*
  Schuester, Terri, 29, *31*
  Schuester, Will, 6, 23, 27–28, *28*
  St. James, Jesse, 38
  Sylvester, Sue (coach), 59, 61–62, *62*
Charity, 82
Cheerios, 59
Chenoweth, Kristin, 64, *64*
Child Hunger Ends Here, 82
Colfer, Chris, 7, 49–54, *51, 52*
Comic-Con, 18–19
Creators. *See* Brennan, Ian; Falchuk, Brad; Murphy, Ryan
Criss, Darren, 54
Critics, opinions of, 17–18

D
De Loreto, Dante, 61
"Don't Stop Believin'", 8, 18

E
Ellis, Brad, 43, *43*

F
Facebook, 20
Falchuk, Brad, 9, 13–16, *14, 15,* 23

99

Fans, 6, 21
 See also Popularity
Fiddler on the Roof, 38
First season, 14, 20, 21
FOX, acceptance of show, 16

G
Gallagher, John, Jr., *39*
Geeks, universality of, 8, 18
Gilsig, Jessalyn, *13,* 29–32
Glee clubs, 26, *26*
 See also New Directions
Glee, overview of, 6
The Glee Project, 80
Gleeks, 6, 21
Groff, Jonathan, 38, *39,* 40
Guest, Christopher, 61
Guest stars, 64, *64*

H
Hairspray (Broadway production), 25
Harrow School (London, England), 26
Harvard Glee Club, 26, *26*
Homosexuality, 53, 54, 62

J
Journey (band), 8, 18

L
Lynch, Jane, 6–7, 8, 59, 60, *60,* 62, 63

M
Marketing, 18–20, *19,* 22, *22, 51*
Mays, Jayma, *33,* 33–34
McCartney, Paul, 8
McHale, Kevin, *55,* 55–56

Michele, Lea, *19,* 35–45, *36, 39, 41, 44*
Les Miserables, 35–36, 39, 40
Monteith, Cory, 72–73, *74, 76,* 78
Morris, Heather, 67–69, *68*
Morrison, Matthew, 23–29, *25, 28*
Murphy, Ryan, 9, 11–13, *12,* 14, *14*
 on character for Colfer, 53
 Gilsig and, 30
 Groff and, 38
 on Michele, 42
 Morrison and, 23, 27
 music choices, 21
 on providing opportunities for new talent, 83
 Riley and, 48
 Sylvester and, 61
Music
 hit songs, 54
 Lynch and, 62
 performed at White House Easter, 69
 popularity, 21
 as promotional platform, 7–8
 relationship to story line, 21
 rules about, 15–16
Musical television shows, 16

N
New Directions, 6, 23, 42, 46, 77
Nip/Tuck, 11, 13, 30

O
O'Malley, Mike, 50, *50*
Online marketing, 20

Orange County High School of the Arts (OCHSA), 24

P
Perry, Katy, 54
Pilot program, 17–18, 20
Pipe Dreams (Salling), 82
Popularity, 6, 7
  competition and, 80
  first season, 20, 21
  music, 21
  tours, 22

R
Riley, Amanda, 46, *47*, 48–49
Rivera, Naya, 70–71, *71*

S
Salling, Mark, 78, *79*, 80–82
Show choirs, 26, 32
Show tours, 22, *22*, *51*
Shum, Harry, Jr., 77, *77*
Smoke Signals (Salling), 82
Spring Awakening
  Michele and, 37, 38, *39*, 39–40
  Ushkowitz and, 58

T
"Teenage Dream," 54
Time magazine lists, 45, 53
Tisch School of the Arts, 24
Twitter, 20

U
Ulrich, Robert, 72, 75
Up with People, 26
Ushkowitz, Jenna, 44, *57*, 57–58, 64

W
William McKinley High School, 8, 20
Writing process, 14

Y
Young Americans, 26

Picture Credits

Cover photo: © Photos 12/Alamy
Adam Rose/Fox-TV/The Kobal Collection/Art Resource, NY, 68
© Allstar Picture Library/Alamy, 77
Barry Brecheisen/Getty Images for Fox, 19
© Bettmann/Corbis, 26
Carin Baer/Fox-TV/The Kobal Collection/Art Resource, NY, 7
Charley Gallay/Getty Images for Fox, 16-17
Chris Cuffaro/Fox-TV/The Kobal Collection/Art Resource, NY, 31, 57, 74
David Livingston/Getty Images, 10, 14
Fox-TV/The Kobal Collection/Art Resource, NY, 33, 64, 70
Jason LaVeris/FilmMagic/Getty Images, 15
Jean-Paul Aussenard/WireImage/Getty Images, 12
Jo Hale/Getty Images, 22
Jordan Strauss/WireImage/Getty Images, 44
Lawrence Lucier/Getty Images, 25
Matthias Clamer/Fox-TV/The Kobal Collection/Art Resource, NY, 41, 52
Patrick Ecclesine/Fox-TV/The Kobal Collection/Art Resource, NY, 79
© Photos 12/Alamy, 28, 36, 43, 47, 50, 55, 62, 66
Robert Pitts/Landov, 51
Stephen Lovekin/WireImage for PMK/HBH/Getty Images, 39
Steve C. Mitchell/EPA/Landov, 76
Suzanne Tenner/Warner Bros/The Kobal Collection/Art Resource, NY, 60

About the Author

Carla Mooney is the author of several books and articles for young readers. She loves investigating and learning about little-known people, places, and events in history. A graduate of the University of Pennsylvania, Mooney lives in Pittsburgh, Pennsylvania, with her husband and three children.

Jay Stream Middle School